# VICIOUS DADDY

BOSTON MAFIA DONS

BIANCA COLE

# CONTENTS

| | | |
|---|---|---|
| 1. Alicia | | 1 |
| 2. Niall | | 13 |
| 3. Alicia | | 23 |
| 4. Niall | | 33 |
| 5. Alicia | | 47 |
| 6. Niall | | 57 |
| 7. Alicia | | 65 |
| 8. Niall | | 81 |
| 9. Alicia | | 89 |
| 10. Niall | | 101 |
| 11. Alicia | | 113 |
| 12. Niall | | 123 |
| 13. Alicia | | 133 |
| 14. Niall | | 143 |
| 15. Alicia | | 155 |
| 16. Niall | | 165 |
| 17. Alicia | | 175 |
| 18. Niall | | 185 |
| 19. Alicia | | 195 |
| 20. Niall | | 207 |
| 21. Alicia | | 217 |
| 22. Niall | | 227 |
| 23. Alicia | | 237 |
| 24. Niall | | 245 |
| 25. Alicia | | 255 |
| 26. Niall | | 263 |
| 27. Alicia | | 275 |

28. Niall 287
　Epilogue 299

*Also by Bianca Cole* 309
*About the Author* 313

Vicious Daddy Copyright © 2021 Bianca Cole

All Rights Reserved.
No part of this publication may be reproduced, stored, or transmitted in any form or by any means, electronic, mechanical, photocopying, recording, scanning, or otherwise without written permission from the publisher. It is illegal to copy this book, post it to a website, or distribute it by any other means without permission.

This novel is entirely a work of fiction. The names, characters and incidents portrayed in it are the work of the author's imagination. Any resemblance to actual persons, living or dead, events or localities is entirely coincidental.

Warning: the unauthorized reproduction or distribution of this copyrighted work is illegal. Criminal copyright infringement, including infringement without monetary gain, is investigated by the FBI and is punishable by up to 5 years in prison and a fine of $250,000.

Book cover design by: Deliciously Dark Designs

Photography: Wander Aguiar Photography

1

## ALICIA

The concrete beneath my head is hard and unforgiving. Even so, it's far more comforting than the soft beds in our foster home. This underpass feels safer than the hell we ran away from. It feels safer than anywhere we've been in a long while because it's just the two of us. No grown-ups to harm us.

Malachy is lying next to me, writhing in his sleep as he so often does. I couldn't protect him the way he protects me.

"Hey," I hear someone whisper, making my heart skip a beat.

Malachy always tells me not to speak to anyone on the streets, but out of intrigue, I glance in the voice's direction. A tall, slim boy who must be a similar age to Malachy stands nearby, holding two pillows and a blanket. "Do you mind if I join you guys? I'll swap a pillow."

I glance over at Malachy, who is still fast asleep. Malachy won't be happy. I glance back at the boy and notice the fear in his eyes. He's like us—scared and alone. I shrug. "Okay, only if I get the pillow though."

He smiles at me and it's friendly—somehow I know that he's just a lost child like we are with no one to take care of him. I watch as he sits close to me and passes me the pillow, which I prop under my head. "Thanks. What's your name?" I ask.

"Niall, little lass, what's yours?"

I swallow hard as Malachy always tells me not to tell strangers my name. "Alicia."

He holds out a hand to me. "It's nice to meet you, Alicia." He tilts his head to the side. "How old are you?"

"Eight years old." I twiddle my thumbs in my lap. "How old are you?"

"Eleven." He yawns, which makes me yawn. "I'm exhausted." He pulls the blanket he'd been holding around himself and places a pillow under his head. "Who is your friend?"

I shake my head. "He's not my friend. Malachy is my brother."

He sighs, as if relieved. "I'm glad he's family. There are real creeps on the streets."

My brow furrows, as I don't understand what he

means. Before I can ask him, Malachy cries out in his sleep, making me jump.

He bolts upright, and I move to comfort him, knowing that he's having a nightmare again. "It's okay, brother. I'm here," I murmur.

Malachy's eyes are wild and frantic. But once he finds my face, he immediately calms down. It only takes him a second to notice the boy I allowed to sleep here. "Who the fuck are you?" he spits, jumping to his feet and pulling out the switch knife he stole from our foster parents.

"Malachy, stop," I say, jumping to my feet and placing a hand on his arm.

"Stay out of this, Alicia." Malachy's shoulders are tense as he steps forward with nasty intentions. I've witnessed the violence my brother is capable of.

Niall jumps to his feet too, backing away with his hands up in surrender. "I don't want any trouble."

"You should have thought about that before stepping into our territory." Malachy thrusts the knife at Niall.

"Stop, Malachy," I cry, but it is no use.

Malachy will not stop. Niall blocks my brother's attack with his pillow and the inner stuffing puffs into the air like snow as it flutters between them. As I helplessly watch, I wonder if my brother could stab an innocent boy—a boy like us.

Footsteps behind me catch my attention, and I turn around to see a man leaning against the pillar of the underpass, staring at me. The look in his eyes gives me the creeps. "What's going on here then, love?" he asks.

I swallow hard. "A fight," I say, turning my attention back to my brother, who no longer has the knife but is fist fighting with Niall.

Boys are so stupid. Niall wasn't threatening either of us. "I bet their fighting after a pretty little thing like you."

I glance back at the man who has got closer now, staring at me in a way that scares me. "Stay back," I mutter, my voice quiet and fragile.

He chuckles. "Not when you are free for the taking." He reaches for me, and I try to step away, but he's too fast.

"Get off—" Before I can shout loud enough, he places his hand over my mouth. I struggle against him, but he's too strong. He drags me away from my brother.

Niall looks up, and our eyes meet. He shoves Malachy so hard that he falls to the ground before running toward me. "Let her go, you bastard," he shouts, balling his fists at the man who is twice his size.

The man doesn't stop. Instead, he laughs. "I'd love to see a little kid like you stop me."

Niall launches himself at the guy, tackling him from the waist. I roll over as he loses his grip on me, knocking my head against the ground. "Ouch," I say, placing a hand where my head hit the concrete.

Niall punches the man over and over, pounding him hard with his fists. Blood coats his knuckles until Malachy finally stops him, grabbing his arm and dragging him away. "That's enough, lad," Malachy says, his aggression toward this boy instantly gone. "You saved my sister." He shakes his head before holding a hand out to him. "I'm sorry about the fight back there, but you can never be too careful on the streets."

Niall stares at his hand for a few moments before taking it and shaking. "Not to worry, name is Niall. Before you pulled a knife on me, I had struck a bargain with your sister there."

Malachy turns to me and helps me to my feet. "Are you hurt?"

I shake my head. "No, thankfully neither is Niall." I shoot him an angry glare for not listening to me. "Thank you for saving me," I say, looking at Niall.

He smiles kindly. "You're welcome, little lass."

"What was this bargain you made then, Alicia?" Malachy asks.

I shrug. "Niall wanted to sleep with us is all, in exchange for a pillow." I point at the pillow next to where Malachy had been sleeping.

Malachy glances at Niall, who shrugs. "I saw you guys and thought you were similar age to me." He swallows hard. "It ain't easy being alone on the streets, especially not at night."

The man Niall beat up groans.

"Shit, well, you best stick with us, lad." Malachy pats him on the shoulder. "We need to find a place to rest tonight and get out of here before he wakes up." Malachy gathers our few belongings hurriedly and I pick up the pillow, offering it back to Niall, since Malachy sliced open his other pillow.

He holds up his hand. "You keep it, Alicia."

I hug it close to me and smile at the young boy who came to my rescue. "Thanks."

Niall shakes his head. "It's nothing." He nods. "Come on now, follow your brother."

I follow Malachy out of the underpass, hugging the pillow tightly as we search for a safe place to sleep, far away from the evil man that tried to take me.

Even though I don't know the boy behind me, I feel safer knowing he's around in addition to Malachy. Life on the streets is hard, and we've only been out here a few weeks. If we want to survive, we need to stop trying to go it alone.

---

*Present Day...*

I walk along the riverside toward our mansion. It's often hard to believe all that Malachy has accomplished, especially considering where we started out.

Many people wouldn't call building a criminal empire an accomplishment, but I sure as hell do. I'm proud of the man my brother became after his terrible upbringing. Malachy has had it hard since the day he was born.

Niall has stuck through thick and thin with him ever since they struck up a friendship in that underpass. He's turned into a viciously protective, gorgeous man that I so often fantasize about. Not that there is anything between us, he's just my brother's gorgeous friend. I sometimes can't believe he's the same scrawny kid I met thirty years ago.

It's a cool spring evening as the darkness shrouds me. I wish I had left the diner half an hour ago, but I got carried away, catching up with Jane, an old friend. I suggested she go on a date with my brother, which she wasn't sure about, but I know the real challenge is Malachy agreeing to meet her. The river walk isn't lit at night and a lot of creeps like to hang out down here. I hug my coat tighter around me and hasten my steps, feeling uneasy.

The crunch of a branch behind me forces me to glance over my shoulder. A dark figure is walking at a startling speed toward me. I hasten my steps, feeling my stomach churn with nausea. Malachy always tells me not to take this shortcut at night, and I'm regretting not listening to him. It's at least double the distance to take the roads, but at least they are well lit and safer.

"Wait up, sweetie," the guy following me calls out. "I only want to talk."

*Fuck.*

I break into a jog, knowing full well this guy does not want to talk. Years living on the streets taught me harsh and unforgiving lessons, but I always had Malachy and Niall to protect me. We used to call ourselves the three musketeers until we grew out of it.

The thud of heavy footsteps following me sends my adrenaline sky high. I sprint faster, trying to put some distance between us. It's no use. The guy is too fast for me as I'm wearing high heels which are not made to run in.

He grabs my shoulder and pulls me to a stop, forcing me against his chest. "I have caught you, sweetie," he sneers, his disgusting, foul breath hitting my face. "Now, the question is, how am I going to use you?"

"Get the fuck off me, you piece of shit," I cry. I try to break free from his grasp, but he's too strong. My mind runs wild with ideas, sorting through my best options.

I scream loud, hoping someone close by might hear me.

The guy slams his hand over my mouth. "Shut your mouth, whore."

An icy dread slices through me, taking me right back to my childhood. Only this time, I don't have anyone here to protect me. My heart pounds against my rib cages as I try to gain control of the fear taking hold of my limbs.

*Think, Alicia. Think.*

I get one of my arms free of his grasp as I hear him unzip his pants. Quickly, I punch him in the balls.

"Motherfucker," he growls, letting go of my other arm and giving me a chance to break free. I don't look back. Instead, I kick my shoes off and leave them, running as fast as I can on bare feet. Pain slices through them as I probably ran over glass. I ignore the pain, knowing what that bastard will do to me will be so much worse.

The thud of fast footsteps behind me makes me lose all hope. I feel tears flooding down my face as I run even faster. "Help," I scream, clutching to the off chance that someone might hear me.

He catches me around the waist and hoists me off the ground. "You are going to pay for that, bitch," he spits, forcing me onto my back on the floor. He unzips his pants and holds me against the ground with his body weight, leering over me.

"Stop," I cry, writhing against his heavy weight and trying not to breathe in his foul, unwashed stench.

I feel helpless, as helpless as I felt every time Malachy had to protect me when we were children. He sacrificed far too much of his childhood to save me. A deed I've never been able to repay him for. At thirty-eight years old, I still can't protect myself.

The thud of approaching footsteps catches my attention and hope coils through me. The man forces my dress up my hips and pulls down my panties when someone pulls him off me. A crunch of bone fills the air as my savior punches him in the face. It's too dark for me to see who has come to my rescue. Punch after punch punctuates the air until the man who tried to rape me is out, cold and lifeless.

I can barely see what is happening, but my rescuer forces the body toward the river's edge. The splash following suggests that he just dumped his body in the river, killing him for sure. I know I should be concerned that a guy just got murdered, but scum like him don't deserve to live. After living a long while on the streets, your morals change and warp into something different.

I hear heavy breathing from the man who came to my rescue. A man I still can't make out as I lie still on the ground. "It's alright now, little lass."

My heart practically stops beating at the sound of Niall's voice. Tears well in my eyes and flood down my cheeks. "Niall?"

He lifts me from the ground, pulling my dress down for me. "Aye, Ali. I heard you scream and came as fast as I could." He presses a kiss to my forehead. "You're safe now."

"What about the man?" I ask.

He tenses against me and in the very dim moonlight I can see a tortured expression on his face. "He will never hurt you or anyone else again."

I relax in his arms. It should unnerve me that Niall just killed to protect me, but it doesn't. After everything we went through on the streets, nothing he or my brother does shocks me. I allow the warmth of his body to penetrate through me. "Thank you," I say, my voice quiet.

"Don't mention it," he murmurs, his voice rough and deep. "Let's get you home." He sets me down on my feet and pulls me tight against him.

"Niall?" I whisper his name.

He looks down at me, and those piercing blue eyes hold an emotion that knocks the air from my lungs. It looks like desire. "What is it?"

"Please don't tell Malachy about this." I shake my head. "He always tells me not to take this way at night, and he will lock me up if he knows."

Niall chuckles softly. "I think you are exaggerating. Malachy wouldn't lock you up."

I bite my lip, knowing that Niall doesn't know how far my brother will go to keep me safe. Although he has been there on the streets with us through almost everything, he doesn't know the lengths Malachy went to in order to keep me safe in that foster home. Malachy never speaks of it, and he hates me telling people. As far as I'm aware, Niall doesn't know about it. My brother is unhinged. Something like this could tip him over the edge. "Please don't tell him, Niall."

He tilts his head slightly. "Are you begging me, little lass?" he asks, an amused smirk on his handsome face.

I narrow my eyes at him. "Yes, just tell me you will keep this between us."

He looks at me for a few beats before nodding. "Aye, don't worry, it will be our secret." He winks, making my heart rate speed up. I've had a little crush on my brother's best friend ever since we grew up. He went from the scrawny, tall boy to a gorgeous, tattooed man that's hard not to notice. "Now come on, Malachy is out."

I sigh heavily, knowing that Malachy is probably at one of those awful auctions he attends. Dark demons haunt my brother—demons that he can't seem to overcome. I wish he would wake up and realize he deserves to be loved.

2

## NIALL

*Two months later....*
I'm distracted by her beautiful singing voice on the way to the kitchen—the voice of an angel.

Alicia is sitting in the library with a book rested on the side of the couch, staring up at the ceiling and singing a beautiful Celtic song that makes my chest ache for more than one reason. I love the way Alicia cherishes our heritage and ties to Ireland.

I've known Alicia since I was eleven years old. She is the most beautiful woman I've ever met, both inside and out. Ever since she got older, I've noticed her in ways that I shouldn't have. I'd hoped that in time my desire for her would go away, especially if she settled down with a guy and had a family. But that has never happened since Malachy always stands in her way.

Instead, the sick fantasies playing out in my head

have been getting more frequent. Especially after I saved her from that piece of scum who tried to rape her two months ago. I killed him and threw him in the river, losing all control of my rage that night. Alicia witnessed what I'm truly capable of, and yet she didn't bat an eyelid. I know she's well aware of what Malachy and I get up to, but I thought she may have been more shocked to see me kill for her.

Malachy doesn't know what happened because she begged me not to tell him. She insists he would have locked her away if he had known. Malachy would kill me if he knew the way I felt about his sister, as he's ridiculously overprotective of her.

Her brown hair is splayed over her back in gentle waves, and I can see half of her face from her position on the sofa. An angel that I've always wanted to protect, ever since the first day we met. Although my desire to protect her has changed in more ways than one.

When we met, we were children, both let down by the people who should have protected us. Alicia stops singing, making my heart race as she glances right at the doorway where I'm standing.

She smiles that beautiful smile, waving at me. "Hey Niall, how's it going?" she calls casually, totally unaware that I've been watching her.

"Hey Alicia. Fine as always, how are you?" I walk into the room, despite knowing I should stay as far away from her as possible.

She sits up straighter, throwing her hair over her shoulder. "I'm okay. Malachy won't tell me why he's so stressed lately." She smiles at me—the smile she always gives me when she wants me to spill my guts. "Any ideas?"

I run a hand across the back of my neck. "You know I can't tell you anything about the clan's business, Ali."

Alicia pouts at me, making my cock stir instantly. I'm thankful I'm wearing my slack fitting jogging pants and tight boxer briefs that hide my desire for her. "Don't be so uptight and tell me what you guys are dealing with. I hate the way Malachy keeps everything from me as if I'm still eight years old. I'm not a kid anymore."

No, she definitely is not. Alicia is thirty-eight years old now and all woman. I try not to stare at her curvy figure, which practically screams for me to worship with my hands. Her hips are wide and sensual in the tight floral dress she's wearing. It highlights her full breasts, which are on display because of the low neckline.

I clear my throat, trying to focus my mind on anything but the dirty things I want to do to my best friend's sister. It doesn't matter how much I try to stop thinking about her, my mind won't stop playing the sick fantasies of me fucking her in every room of his house.

"Niall?" Alicia says my name, snapping me out of my lust filled daydream.

I shake my head. "You know I shouldn't lass." I walk over to the bookshelf on the far wall and focus my attention on it. Anywhere other than the tempting beauty sitting behind me. It's all I can do to stop myself from losing my mind. I run my hands over the spines of the books, wondering how I'm going to get Alicia out of my system.

A soft hand lands on my shoulder, making me tense. Alicia snuck up on me quieter than a damn mouse. "Please, Niall."

I clench my jaw before turning to face her.

Alicia stares up at me with those stunning emerald eyes of hers. It's as if she knows the hold she has on me. I feel my cock getting hard as my eyes dip to her full, red — lips I'd love to slide my cock through and claim her pretty little throat.

*Fuck.*

I put some distance between us. "It's best you don't know what is going on."

Alicia chases after me and dashes in front of me, setting her hand on my chest. "Come on, Niall. It's me you are talking to."

I glance down at her dainty hand on my chest, wishing I could grab it and pull her against me. All I want is to kiss every inch of her body and make her mine. "Alicia." Her name comes out of me in a tortured rasp. When I meet her gaze, I see the desire dancing in her eyes too.

I've noticed it ever since I saved her that night. A change in the way she is around me. It took my rescue by the river for her to see me the way I've seen her for so many years.

"What have you got to lose?" she asks, tilting her head to the side slightly.

*Everything.*

If I keep indulging Alicia and letting her know clan secrets behind Malachy's back, then I may as well fuck her. She has a way of getting under my skin and forcing me to spill my guts. "Malachy doesn't want me to worry you."

"Fuck Malachy and what he wants," she says, her eyes wild. "He can't keep treating me like a fucking kid."

It's true that Malachy does still see Alicia as a defenseless little eight-year-old girl. "Fine, we're having some trouble with the Italians is all."

Her brow furrows. "What kind of trouble?"

I sigh heavily. "Milo Mazzeo blew up Malachy's corvette."

Alicia gasps. "Fuck, I wondered where it was." She shakes her head. "He loved that car. No wonder he's been snappy lately."

I chuckle. "Isn't he snappy always?"

Alicia smiles. "Yeah, but he's been really grumpy."

She licks her bottom lip, drawing my eyes to it. "Does that mean there is going to be a war?"

I sense the concern in her voice and clench my fist to stop myself from wrapping her in my arms and soothing her concerns. "Possibly. No matter what happens, we won't let anything happen to you, little lass."

Alicia's eyes flash with irritation. "I wish you wouldn't call me that."

I can't help but laugh at how adorable she is when she's angry. "Why?"

She sets her hands on her hips, drawing my attention to her full cleavage. "Because I'm not a kid anymore, Niall."

*Don't I know it.*

"Aye, lass. You most certainly are not." I lose my self-control for a moment and when my eyes move back to hers, there's dark and dangerous passion in her expression.

"What is that supposed to mean?" she asks, stepping closer.

I clench my jaw, realizing that I slipped up. "Nothing." I rub my hand across the back of my neck. "I'm just saying you are all grown up, is all."

Her eyes move from mine, down my chest, and down to the bulge in my jogging pants. Alicia's cheeks stain a deep red when she notices the bulge, and her eyes snap back to mine. "You forget you are only three years older than me." She shakes her head. "We were both kids when we met."

I sigh heavily, as it's not entirely true. In terms of our age, there wasn't much difference, but Malachy had protected her innocence. I lost that a long time before we met. My childhood ended when the one person who was supposed to care for me violated me and forced me to run. "Age is a number. When we met, you were still a kid. I wasn't."

Alicia's eyes flash with guilt, and she takes a step back, as she knows exactly what I've been through. She is one of the few people in my life who know about my abusive past. "I know, sorry." She turns away from me. "I just wish Malachy would trust me enough to confide in me, that's all."

I nod in response. "Malachy just wants to protect you."

He has always been possessive of his baby sister. Any man that has ever gone near Alicia, he's scared away, to my relief. I can't imagine watching her with another man. The mere thought sends me into a jealous rage.

"Are you alright?" Alicia asks, her attention on my clenched fists.

I try to chill out, stretching my fingers out. "Yeah, fine." I shake my head. "I've just got a lot on my mind."

Alicia sets her hand on my chest again, making me tense. "Do you want to talk about it?"

I look down at her dainty fingers touching me. All I want to do is grab her hand, pull her close, and kiss her the way I've longed to kiss her for too damn long. My desire is becoming uncontrollable. My gaze moves from her hand to her face. I can't work out if I'm imagining the passion in her gaze or not, as I move my attention to her lips. Maybe I'm finally losing it. She licks them, making the temptation almost unbearable.

"Niall?" she murmurs my name. Alicia appears to lean closer and for a moment, so do I. The tension in the air heightened as we both stare into each other's eyes, lost in a daydream that can never come true.

The crash of someone dropping something outside jolts me out of the daydream we'd fallen prey to. "Not much to talk about," I say, stepping away so her hand falls to her side. "It was nice chatting, little lass. Don't ask me about anymore inside information though." I wink at her to diffuse the tension charging through the air. "You've got all you're going to get from me."

A flash of hurt enters her stunning green eyes. I try not to let it affect me. Alicia needs to understand that I'm her brother's second-in-command, first and foremost.

"I'll see you around, little lass," I say, turning away from her and walking out of the library without a backward glance. Every moment I spend near her, it is becoming harder to cage the burning desire dominating my actions when she is close.

I need to stay away from her. She's my best friend's baby sister, and Malachy and I may be close, but fucking Alicia may be a step too far. Alicia has always been the one person he covets and protects with his life, and I don't like my chances if I fall into his bad books.

3

## ALICIA

*I* wait by the front door, knowing that my brother is going out. I saw Niall pull up Malachy's car in front of the house. My brother rarely goes out. The only time he does is when he's going to one of those barbaric virgin auctions. It's about time I intervened in his sick ways once and for all. He's forty-two years old.

He needs to find a girl to settle down with, although I guess I can't talk since I haven't settled down myself. It doesn't help that Malachy always chases away any guy I'm interested in. I stopped bothering bringing men home years ago.

Malachy marches toward the door and doesn't notice me until the very last moment.

"What are you doing, Sis?" he asks, brow furrowing.

I shrug, as I know Malachy hates being told what

to do. My questioning him about his actions won't go down too well. "Are you going to one of those terrible auctions again?"

Malachy's jaw tenses. I know he hates that I'm aware of his penchant for virgins and buying them, but he's not exactly discreet about it. He's messed up from our childhood, or lack of it. I wish he would realize that he deserves to be happy, despite the shit he went through in the past.

"What does it matter?" He asks, looking frustrated.

I sigh, knowing that he's never going to change his ways. It makes me feel guilty as half the terrible things he went through were to protect me. "Why don't you give my friend Jane a chance and go on one date?"

There's a flash of amusement in Malachy's eyes at the suggestion. "Believe me, little sis. Your friend wants nothing to do with me." I know that may well be true. The bruises that the virgins he buys often have on them scare me. By the time he's through with them, they're empty shells floating through the hallway of our home. I wonder if he would treat Jane that way. Malachy leans toward me and kisses my cheek. "Don't wait up." Before I have the chance to protest, he walks out of the front door.

"I'd give up on that one if I were you," Niall says from behind, startling me.

I swallow hard and turn to face my brother's best friend, who is the epitome of a gorgeous bad boy. Six foot four of pure muscle and covered in tattoos, he's a world away from the scrawny boy that approached us that night while sleeping in the underpass. I shake my head. "He needs to settle down and find a girl to marry, not buy a virgin every couple of months."

Niall laughs. "The guy is as stubborn as hell, Ali. There's no way he's settling down soon."

My stomach churns at hearing him call me Ali. He's the only person who does. A silence falls between us as we stare into each other's eyes. An unmistakable tension floods the air between us as I feel myself lost in his ice-blue stare. I lick my lips as the nerves inside of me surge. Everything has been different between us lately.

Desperate to break the tension, I clear my throat. "What are you up to tonight?" I ask, instantly regretting asking him when I realize it sounds like I want to hang out.

"Not much." There's a brief silence between us. "Do you want to watch a movie?"

My brow furrows as Niall never asks me to spend time with him. "I thought you'd have a hot date on a Friday night." I wink at him playfully, even though inside, green envy flows through my veins. He's often out on the weekend, no doubt picking up women at bars. We've known each other since we were children and never once has Niall had a steady girlfriend.

He laughs that deep, rumbling laugh that sends

goosebumps over my skin. "Yeah, a hot date with you," he says, shrugging. "We can order pizza."

It's pathetic, the way my stomach dances with butterflies when I hear him say he has a hot date with me. I know he's joking.

As I stare into his eyes, I know this is a bad idea. Lately, I can't stop thinking about him in ways I shouldn't think about my brother's best friend. Ever since he saved me from that bastard two months ago, Niall has become a bit of an obsession. I think about him all the time and it's getting worse with each day that passes. He's always looked out for me, ever since the first day we met.

"Okay," I say, smiling to hide my reluctance. "Let's raid the kitchen for snacks and alcohol."

Niall laughs. "Sounds like a good plan, little lass."

I can't understand why my stomach flips every time he calls me that. It makes me hot under the collar. "Great." I walk past him toward the kitchen, feeling my heart race in my chest. An entire evening spent with a man I've been having questionable urges toward for the past two months is a terrible idea.

I can sense him following me as I lead the way to the kitchen. Once I enter, I head straight for the fridge in search of wine. "I guess you'll want beer, right?" I ask.

He smiles that unbelievably handsome smile and nods. "You know me so well, lass."

I shake my head and pull out a six-pack of beer. "Six enough?"

He rubs a hand across his neat beard. "Between us or just for me?"

"Just for you." I pull a bottle of white wine out of the rack in the fridge. "I'll stick with wine."

He nods. "Then six will be enough." Niall rubs a hand across the back of his neck. "At least until the pizza arrives."

Ever since the day in the library two weeks ago, there's been a tension between us I can practically feel in the air. It's full of unbridled passion and forbidden desire that neither of us knows how to quench. Both of us spending the night alone and drinking alcohol probably isn't the best idea.

"Check out what snacks we've got," I say, glancing at the cupboard next to him.

Niall opens the door and pulls out a bag of Cool Ranch Doritos. "Your favorite."

I smile and walk over to him, grabbing them from his hand. "And all mine, you better get your own."

Niall shakes his head. "That's greedy, little lass." He rustles in the cupboard and pulls out another bag of chips for himself.

I shrug. "I've got a good appetite." Leading the way, I walk down the corridor toward the movie room. Niall's presence close behind me is ever apparent. His masculine scent of musk overwhelms the air, making my knees weak. Niall's eyes are on me as I can practically feel them burning a hole into my back.

The tension is higher than ever. It all started when he saved me from that rapist. There was a change in the dynamic between us. It's why spending the night together watching a movie is a stupid idea. Despite neither of us acknowledging the chemistry between us, it's clear that we both want each other in ways we shouldn't.

Malachy isn't exactly the most understanding brother. Although I'm a full-grown woman, he still sees me as this little girl he needs to protect from everyone, including men. It's one reason I've never really had a steady relationship, since Malachy chases prospective partners away.

Instead, I'm a member of Euphoria in Boston. An exclusive sex-club I've been going to for a while now. Malachy would kill me if he knew, but I make sure he could never find out.

"What movie do you want to watch?" Niall asks, flopping down on the sofa in front of the TV and grabbing the remote.

"I've wanted to watch Lawless for a while." I glance at him. "You up for that?"

He smirks. "The only reason a girl ever wants to watch that movie is because they have the hots for Hardy."

I laugh and hold my hands up in surrender. "Well, he is hot." Although, *not as hot as you*. There's no way

I'd admit that out loud, but it's impossible to stop my mind from thinking it. Niall has always been hot since he was sixteen years old, but the older he got, the hotter he became. Especially as he filled out and started getting tattoos. I shrug. "But, I've heard it's an excellent film."

He stares at me for a few moments before nodding. "Sure, why not?"

I sit next to him, and he selects the movie, hitting play. My heart is pounding in my chest as I'm painfully aware of him so close to me. The warmth of his body radiates toward me, making me long to move closer.

I fold my arms over my chest and lean back into the plush cushions of the couch, trying to focus on the movie as it plays. The tension in the room makes it almost impossible to breathe. Ever since the night by the river, there's been a shift in our relationship. I can't work out if it's just my imagination or whether he wants this as badly as I do.

I grab the bag of chips and open them, knowing the only way to keep my mind off of the six-foot-four, muscled and tattooed god sitting next to me is to stuff my face.

Niall reaches for the bag and grabs one, smirking at me. "You can't eat that entire bag yourself."

I narrow my eyes at him and snatch the chip back, shoving it in my mouth. "I can and I will. Keep your hands to yourself." The remark ignites something dark in his eyes that makes my stomach churn.

He laughs. "What about the pizza?"

I shake my head. "You clearly don't know me very well if you don't know how much I can eat."

His eyes flash with an emotion I can't quite place. "I know you well enough, little lass."

I can't understand the intensity in his gaze and why it makes me slick between my thighs. He holds my gaze and the apprehension between us crackles in the air. For a moment, I'm lost in the depth of his ice-blue irises, overpowered by a craving that no amount of chips or pizza can overcome. It feels like forever passes by until Niall finally breaks the passionate tension, clearing his throat and glancing at the screen on the wall.

I force my attention from his flawless face and onto the movie, which has started. Niall's invitation to watch a movie tonight is dangerous. Unless I'm insane, we both want to cross a line that we should never cross. We've known each other our entire lives, and Malachy is his best friend.

The worry isn't just how angry Malachy would be about it, but he's harmed men that got too close to me. I can't subject Niall to that danger, no matter how close they are. Neither of us could be sure what Malachy's reaction would be to his baby sister and best friend fucking.

He knows Niall better than he knows anyone.

There's no chance in hell Niall would ever hurt me. The problem is the same can't be said for what Malachy might do to him. I won't risk his life over a silly crush, no matter how badly I want the man sitting by my side. His blood would be on my hands if we crossed the line and Malachy found out and took it badly.

4

NIALL

Alicia sits precariously close to me on the couch, and it's impossible not to keep replaying my dirty vision of her bent over the coffee table, naked and panting while I fuck her. She wanted to watch *Lawless,* a movie I love, and yet I've barely paid attention to a fucking second of it.

*Shit.*

Why the hell did I ask to her to watch a movie with me tonight?

I knew full well Malachy was out of the house, which only makes the temptation more difficult to resist. Her scent overwhelms the air, and it makes it impossible to focus.

"Do you reckon that's even physically possible?" Alicia asks, looking right at me and catching me off guard.

My brow furrows. "What?"

"In the movie." She points at the screen. "The character Hardy plays said he walked with a slit throat twelve miles."

Thankfully, I've seen the movie before, so I know what she is talking about. "Nah, keep watching and you'll find out what really happened."

She sighs. "I honestly thought he was dead." Her brow furrows. "Wait, have you seen it before?"

I laugh. "Yeah, why?"

She shoves me in the arm gently. "You should have said, no wonder you aren't paying any attention." She hits pause. "Where is that damn pizza? I'm starving."

I shrug and dig my cell phone out of my pocket, pulling up the tracker on my phone. "Apparently it's on the way."

Alicia groans. "I'm so fucking hungry."

I bite my lip, as I'm not hungry for food at all right now. My cock is painfully hard, as I can't get the image of Alicia wrapping her plump, perfect lips around it out of my mind. All I'm hungry for is devouring the woman sitting next to me—a woman that is one hundred percent off limits.

I take a long gulp of my beer. "I'll ring them and check how long they'll be." I hit the number for the pizza place we ordered from, and it rings before cutting off on the busy dial tone. "Shit, the line is busy. You can't be that hungry; you've eaten a whole family size bag of Doritos."

She narrows her eyes at me. "And drank an entire bottle of wine. When I drink, it makes me hungry."

The girl downed that wine so fucking fast I hardly noticed her bottle was empty. It means Alicia is drunk, and I'm not exactly sober either.

She leans over me and grabs my can of beer from my hand, taking a swig. "Sharing is caring."

God, she does not want to know what I want to share with her right now. My cock is practically straining against my pants, desperate to break free. Alicia's hand brushes against my crotch and my cock throbs.

"Alicia," I say her name in warning, narrowing my eyes.

She can't find out how badly I want her. We already came too close to crossing a line in the library two weeks ago. "What? I've run out of wine."

I sigh heavily and pull a can from the six-pack she got me. "Here, have your own."

She sits up straighter and takes the can, opening it. "Thanks."

I watch as she takes a long sip, unable to keep my eyes off her lips. Lips I can't stop thinking about kissing.

Someone clears their throat behind us, making me jump. I glance around to see Sasha, the maid, holding our pizzas. "The delivery guy just dropped your food off."

I stand and approach her. "Thanks, Sasha."

Her brow furrows as she glances at Alicia on the sofa. "No problem. How are you?" She asks, twirling her fingers in the end of her hair.

I grit my teeth. "I'm fine." Sasha has constantly flirted with me since she started working here six months ago. She's beautiful, but I can't think of any other girl in that way. Alicia has been under my skin for too many years. She's the object of all my fantasies. It's the reason I always shoot Malachy's invites to those messed up auctions down.

"Can I get you anything else?" Sasha asks, batting her eyelids at me.

"No, thanks." I turn my back on her and return to sit next to Alicia on the sofa. When I glance back, she has left us.

"I think Sasha wants you," Alicia says, taking a long swig of beer.

I run a hand through my hair. "Yeah, well, I don't want her."

Alicia's brow furrows. "Why not? She's beautiful."

I can't believe she is even asking me this. Alicia is so blind to the way I feel about her it's ridiculous. Malachy's overzealous protection of his baby sister is the only reason I haven't acted on my feelings all these years. "Because I want someone else," I say, holding her gaze possessively. If she doesn't realize by now that I want her, she's fucking oblivious.

Alicia's throat bobs. "Oh." She twirls the end of

her long, dark hair around her finger nervously. "Who?"

I feel an irritated growl rumble through my chest. "Isn't it obvious?"

Her skin flushes pink, and she avoids my gaze and reaches for one of the pizza boxes. I grab her arm before she can reach it. "Alicia." Her name sounds like a curse from my lips.

Alicia's eyes meet mine. "What?"

I clench my jaw, knowing the dangerous line I'm flirting with. "You didn't answer my question. Isn't it obvious who I want?" We can't keep doing this dance around each other.

Alicia glances down at my hand wrapped tightly around her arm before meeting my gaze again. "Niall," she breathes my name in a plea and a warning. She knows we shouldn't do this. "The pizza will go cold."

"Fuck the pizza, little lass," I growl, feeling my urges surge to the surface. One thing I've learned is that the longer I fight the desperate need to claim Alicia, the more difficult it becomes to keep a leash on the heavy desire building inside of me. "Answer the question."

Alicia yanks her arm free and stands. "I don't know." She snatches the pizza off the table and turns to leave. "Now I'm going to go eat my goddamn pizza in peace."

Scorching rage floods my vision as I move swiftly

after her. Before she makes it to the door, I grab her hips. "Stop pushing me, little lass."

Alicia tenses against me as I pull her back against my chest. "Niall, what are you—"

I grab the pizza box out of her hand and set it down on the sideboard nearby. "I want you to answer my question."

"Answer it yourself, dickhead," she spits.

I press my lips against her nape. "You, Alicia," I breathe, knowing I can't take it back now. It's time to stop hiding and face up to what I want—my best friend's sister.

All the air escapes her lungs on a breath as she tries to fight away from me. "Niall, you know we can't—"

"Bullshit. Malachy's out," I cut in before she can tell me we can't do it because of her brother. "He'll never know."

Alicia's breaths come out in shaky rasps that cut right to my cock. It's an erotic sound that makes it difficult not to bend her over with the door open and fuck her for all the staff to see. "Niall, I don't think we should."

I growl softly and pull her away from the door, keeping her back pressed against me. "Stop thinking and just feel, baby girl," I murmur, nibbling the shell of her ear softly. I reach for the door and push it shut. Malachy should be out for a few more hours, but I'd rather not take any risks.

Alicia shudders against me, arching her back instinctively. "This is a terrible idea."

"A terribly good idea, little lass." I move my lips to her neck and kiss her there, making her moan. All sense of rhyme and reason is lost. It turns out fighting your instincts for years doesn't make them go away, it deepens the ravenous hunger. I spin her around to face me and capture her lips for the first time.

It feels like my world spins as I lose myself in her heady, feminine scent. My tongue delves into her mouth, claiming it fully and completely. Her tongue tangles with mine, proving to me she wants this as badly as I do.

Alicia moans into my mouth, making my balls tighten.

"Fuck, I've wanted to kiss you for so damn long," I murmur against her lips, wishing that I'd crossed the line before this moment. The pent-up desire burning inside of me is almost unbearable. It makes it hard to control my vicious tendencies lurking beneath the surface. The last thing I want to do is hurt Alicia.

I wrap my arms tightly around her waist and lift her, carrying her back to the sofa.

Her arms slide tentatively around my neck as she allows me to. "Niall, what are we—"

I silence her with my mouth. I can't hear her reasoning right now, as she might convince me to stop. Gently, I place her down on her back on the sofa. "No questions, little lass. I want you. It's as simple as that."

Her emerald eyes dilate as she watches me pull my shirt over my head. They roam over every inch of my body, taking in the tattoos scrolling over my skin.

"Your turn," I breathe, feeling the anticipation coiling through me.

Alicia hesitates, staring up at me with uncertainty. "What if my brother gets—"

I growl, cutting her off from finishing her sentence. "I said no questions. Do you want me to punish you?"

I'm surprised when I see a flash of lusty excitement pulse in her eyes as she licks her lips. "I just don't want to get caught."

I shake my head. "We won't. Take your top off, or I'll do it for you."

Alicia unbuttons the front of her blouse slowly, holding our eye contact. Finally, once she unbuttons the last one, her blouse falls open, revealing her large breasts in a red lace bra that makes my cock throb. She tosses the blouse on the floor.

"And the bra," I order, barely recognizing my voice.

Alicia raises a brow questioningly but doesn't defy me. Her hand slips behind her back as she unclips the bra, letting it fall to her lap.

I groan at the sight of her nipples, hard and erect, pointing right at me. They're practically begging me to suck them. There's no holding me back anymore as I step toward her. I kneel between her legs on the sofa, cupping her firm breasts in my hands. "Fucking perfect," I muse before lowering my mouth to her right nipple and sucking it into my mouth.

Alicia's hips buck against me, and she gasps, lacing her fingers into my hair. A problem I'll have to fix somehow. I prefer my women restrained, and the desire to restrain Alicia is all-consuming.

I move my lips to her other nipple and suck it into my mouth.

Alicia's moans spur me on as I move my hands to her jeans and unzip them. She grabs my hand to stop me. "Your turn next," she says, looking at me with dilated eyes.

I smirk at her and stand, unzipping my pants and pulling them down.

Alicia gasps the moment I stand up again. "Fuck me," she says.

"That is the intention."

She shakes her head. "You're huge."

I tilt my head to the side, loving the way she's boosting my ego. "Maybe I've got socks stuffed down there."

"Do you?" she asks, entranced by the bulge at my crotch.

"Why don't you come over here and find out?" I ask.

She licks her bottom lip and moves her gaze to my face. "Only if I get a taste."

I raise a brow. "Of course."

Alicia rises from the sofa and walks toward me slowly before dropping to her knees in front of me. It's as if she were born to submit. "Can I?" she asks, looking up at me like a damn angel.

"Yes, baby girl," I breathe, feeling my cock leak in anticipation.

She grabs the waistband of my boxer briefs and pulls them down, revealing my cock. Her gasp only makes me leak more. "So damn big," she marvels, grabbing my shaft with one hand and tugging.

"Fuck," I curse, watching her touch me. "Put it in your mouth," I order.

She opens her mouth and closes her lips around the head of my cock, slowly swirling her tongue around me in teasing strokes.

More precum leaks onto her tongue, making her moan. I try to fight the need to fist her hair in my hands and thrust every inch into the back of her throat, but I can't. The need to dominate her is overwhelming.

I grab hold of her hair and force her throat onto my cock. It's as if Alicia saw it coming as she barely bats an eyelid. Her breathing is impeccable as she manages not to gag as I slide right past her reflex.

"That's it, baby girl, swallow my cock," I growl, propelling my hips in and out as I fuck her throat.

Alicia gags, saliva spilling down her face and tears prickling at her eyes. It's a perfect vision. A scene I'd only ever expected to witness in my perverse dreams.

It's hard to believe that the girl I've craved for is on her knees, taking everything I give her.

Alicia puts her hands on my thighs, trying to gain some kind of control.

I pull my cock from her throat, giving her a chance to catch her breath. "You take my cock perfectly, little lass."

She gazes up at me with a carnal expression that makes me crazy. "You taste so good," she breathes, licking a drop of precum from her lips. "Give me more."

I groan and force my cock through her lips, thrusting into the back of her throat repeatedly.

She takes it like a fucking champ. I feel my balls tighten, realizing I'm getting close. I pull Alicia off me and yank her up from the floor. "My turn to taste you." I lift her and set her down on the sofa, pulling her jeans off of her in one tug.

Alicia clenches her thighs together to hide how drenched she is.

"Open your legs for me," I order.

Alicia's cheeks are deep red as she slowly opens her thighs, allowing me to see her red drenched lace panties.

"Fuck you are wet, Ali," I groan, feeling my cock throb at the sight. I drop to my knees between her thighs and press my nose against her crotch, inhaling her sweet as hell scent. "So damn wet for me," I growl before tearing her panties in two.

Alicia gasps. "Those were expensive."

I don't reply to her as right now I don't give a damn about her expensive lingerie. I'll buy her new ones. I kiss her inner thigh, making her quiver at the light touch. Slowly, I drag my tongue closer to her dripping center.

"Please, Niall," she breathes.

I can't help but smile against her skin, hearing her beg so desperately for me. I glance up at her from between her thighs. "Please, what?" I ask, tilting my head slightly.

She narrows her eyes at me and blows out a frustrated breath. "You know what."

I raise a brow. "I want to hear you tell me what you want, little lass."

Alicia sinks her teeth into her bottom lip before nodding. "I want you to eat me out, you knucklehead."

I grab hold of her thighs hard, putting enough pressure to bruise. "That's not an acceptable way to talk to the man that's going to make you orgasm harder than you've ever orgasmed in your life."

She doesn't flinch at my forceful handling of her. "That's cocky."

I hold her gaze with unwavering confidence. "It's the truth, baby girl and you better believe it."

Her brow furrows. "Prove it."

I growl softly at the challenge. "My pleasure."

Alicia gasps as I bury my tongue in her pussy,

tasting her deeply. She's sweeter than I ever could have imagined. This is what I've been waiting for all these years: Alicia spread and dripping for me, watching me as I devour her. I hold her eye contact as I move my tongue from her perfect cunt to her throbbing clit. The moment my tongue connects with her sensitive spot, she jerks, moaning deeply.

Her fingers claw at the throw on the sofa as I slide two fingers deep into her tight, wet heat. I clench my jaw, trying to still the primal urge to pull my fingers out and slide my cock inside of her instead. Right now, I want to give her mind-blowing pleasure to prove to her I can make her feel better than any man ever has.

"So damn tight, little lass," I groan, thrusting my fingers in and out of her dripping cunt. My thirst for her can't be quenched, no matter how much I taste her. Alicia has haunted my dreams and fantasies for too long. It feels like I'm no longer here, floating above my body as my primitive male instincts take control. "I want you to come for me," I growl, thrusting all four fingers into her tight pussy.

She gasps, her body tensing as her first orgasm hits her. "Fuck, yes," she cries.

I groan at the way her tight pussy clamps around my fingers, drawing them deeper. I pull them out despite her pussy clasping hold of them. My tongue replaces my fingers as I taste every drop of her, savoring her essence. It calls to me in the most primal way, coaxing me to take what I've wanted for so long.

I know this night won't end until I've claimed the forbidden fruit. Alicia is mine. Always has been and always will be.

5

## ALICIA

Niall's teeth graze my clit, and it's all it takes to send me over the edge for the second time in ten minutes. Every part of my body tenses, and then something happens. Something that has never happened before. A rush of pleasure so indescribable, followed by a gush of liquid squirting from my pussy onto Niall's face. It's one of the best feelings I've ever felt, but I feel a mix of shame and confusion over what the hell just happened.

I tense, trying to sit up. "I'm sorry, I don't—"

Niall pushes me back down, looking me right in the eye. "Never apologize for squirting, baby girl, that was hot as sin." Niall brings his head back to my pussy and laps up every drop of my juice as if he's starving for it. "I love it when you squirt for me." His icy-blue eyes look far off and lucid as he loses himself in us.

My nipples harden to painful and my pussy

tightens as my orgasm continues to hold me captive.

Maybe he was right to be cocky. The man is a master with his tongue like no other I've ever experienced. He straightens and fists his straining, rock-hard shaft in his hands. "I think I proved it, don't you?" he asks, eyebrow raised.

I nod, unable to find the words to speak right now.

Niall is a vision of perfection. I take in every dip and curve of his hard muscles veiled in beautiful ink. I've always loved the way his tattoo spreads up his neck, but seeing him totally naked like this emphasizes the beauty of the art on his skin. I want to lick every inch of his body, worshipping it the way it was made to be worshipped.

"Fuck me," I moan, feeling the need deep inside of my core increase as I watch him stroke his perfect cock up and down.

A greedy lust floods his eyes. "You don't have to ask me twice, little lass," he groans, moving forward. He stops suddenly, tilting his head to the side. "First, I need to find something to restrain you with."

My heart skips a beat and the excitement increases.

*Could Niall's taste in sex be as twisted and rough as mine?*

From the way he claimed and fucked my throat so roughly, I hope so. A tingling need pulses through every nerve in my body, consuming me from the inside out. I've wanted no one the way I want Niall.

## VICIOUS DADDY

It's an unbelievable, burning hunger that feels like it could eat me alive if I don't feel him inside of me, completing me.

Niall walks over to the drapes, which are tied back with rope ties. He pulls one off and glances back at me. "This should work nicely." He returns to the sofa and grabs my wrists forcefully, wrapping the tie around both of them and tightening them around my wrist with a knot that I couldn't undo no matter how hard I try.

A flood of jealousy hits me as I wonder who else he's tied up like this. It's ridiculous, as I know Niall has been with many other women. I just hate thinking about it.

"Now you have no control," he breathes, holding my gaze with a harsh look that sends shivers down my spine. "I own you."

My stomach tightens at the possessive tone of his voice.

Niall grabs my hips and forces me to lie down on the sofa at a different angle, allowing him to kneel between my thighs. He strokes the enormous length between his legs, making every part of my body ache for him.

Niall's ice-blue eyes bore into me with an intensity that heats me right to the core. He's a hungry beast, ready to devour me.

"Watch us, baby girl," he orders, making my stomach clench.

I writhe against the rope he used to tie my wrists up, wanting nothing more than to wrap my arms around his neck and pull him inside of me.

I drop my attention to his thick, long cock nudging at my entrance. The need inside of me doubles at the sight. It's so wrong that we're doing this, but it feels right in ways I can't put into words.

The man who has always protected me now wants me. It's too much to get my head around. I always thought Niall saw me as his best friend's useless little sister, even if we are adults now. There's always been this disconnect between Niall and me. I couldn't understand why he kept me at arm's length as we got older until two months ago, when he saved me.

Perhaps what we are doing now is the reason.

"Please, Niall," I moan, feeling my clit throb with need.

A handsome smirk curls onto his lips, making my insides melt. "Since you asked so nicely, lass." He thrusts his hips forward, burying every inch inside of me with one long stroke.

My slick, soaking wet pussy engulfs every single inch until his balls rest against my ass. The moment he's inside of me, I feel complete. The deep ache that pulsed inside of me is soothed by the immense size of his cock. We shouldn't be doing this, and yet it feels utterly right. I watch as he slowly draws his cock out of me, slick with my juices.

"Such a dirty little girl watching me fuck your

pretty little cunt, aren't you?"

My nipples tighten and stomach flutters at his dirty talk. "Niall," I half moan and half gasp, hearing him be so damn dirty.

"That's it, baby girl, moan my name," he growls, before thrusting every inch back inside of me hard.

My back arches and I pull at the rope around my wrists, loving being dominated. "Yes, fuck me," I groan, feeling the pleasure tear through every nerve ending in my body. Niall is a god. He's made me come twice already. I've never come so fast for any man before. Already, I can feel that third orgasm building as he fills and stretches me with his cock.

Niall captures my lips, kissing me viciously. His teeth graze my lip, and he bites softly. "Fuck, little lass, I've wanted you for so long," he groans, fucking me harder still.

I arch my back, wanting him to lose control. The need to be treated so roughly has always confused me. It's the reason I joined Euphoria as it was the one place people wouldn't judge me for my sexual kinks. The possibility that Niall might have similar kinks excites me.

He presses his fingertips into my hips hard enough to bruise, making me moan louder. Niall's eyes flash with a feral desire that makes me feel more wanted than I've felt in my entire life. He grabs hold of my throat, softly at first. It only makes my desire increase.

When I don't tense, he chokes me. I feel my pussy

getting wetter and that overwhelming frenzy inside of me building higher and higher. The lack of oxygen only increases the rush of pleasure mounting inside of me.

Niall knows what he's doing as he backs off at the right time. "Fuck, baby girl, you make me crazy," he groans, thrusting into me so hard it's as if he's trying to break me in two. The need between us is frenzied as he kisses me deeply, continuing to pound into me hard and fast.

Niall grabs my hips suddenly, flipping me onto all fours. He pushes my face into the cushions of the couch roughly, digging his fingertips into my hips. "You take my cock so damn well, little lass." He slowly slides every inch back inside of me, letting me feel him invading my body softly before he turns feral again.

I moan so loudly, forgetting where we are and what we're doing. Any of the staff could hear us, but I can't find it in me to care. It feels so dirty and yet so fucking right. Niall should be off limits. I know that to my very core and yet the same part of me knows how right this is.

Niall's rough treatment of me only makes me want more. He spanks my ass hard, and every muscle in my body tenses. It's as if this man can read my mind. He's a master of my body in every way. He continues to fuck me harder, spanking my ass with the exact right amount of force.

I've never felt so connected to anyone else before in my life. Niall makes me feel wanted and safe, two things I've craved my entire life. It's crazy to think he's been here, right in front of me all this time.

Niall stops, making me whimper. "Lie down again. I want to look into your eyes as you come on my cock," he orders.

I do as he says, flopping down onto my back with my tied arms in front of me. Niall is a vision of perfection. His taught muscles are tense and rippling as he breathes heavily, staring at me with such crazed passion.

The sight of his cock so hard and erect, dripping with precum and my own juice that I want to lick off, feels like torture as he waits, watching me. "Are you ready to come for me, little lass?"

I swallow hard at him using that nickname. A nickname he's given me since I first met him. It feels both wrong and right that he would use it while we fuck. "Yes," I breathe. "I need you to fill me with your seed, Niall," I beg, looking him straight in the eye.

Any hold he had on his senses snaps as he comes at me like a wild animal, thrusting his cock all the way inside until he can't sink any deeper. He bites my neck hard enough to leave a mark, drawing blood. I groan, shocked when he licks the wound. "Oh fuck," I breathe, feeling conquered by him.

Our instincts call to each other, driving us both wilder with need with each move we make.

"You're mine, Alicia. Do you understand?" he murmurs into my ear before biting my earlobe.

"Fuck, yes," I gasp, finding it almost impossible to draw enough oxygen into my lungs.

His huge cock stretches me as he increases the momentum, driving me closer to heaven with each thrust. I can feel the intensity of my orgasm building higher. It's the most amazing sensation I've ever felt.

"I want to feel that pretty little cunt come on my cock, baby girl."

His dirty talk is all it takes to coax a third, world-shattering orgasm from my body. My eyes roll back in my head, as the pleasure is too much to bear. It's a mix between total euphoria and pain. The same sensation hits me as a flood of liquid pools around his cock and squirts onto his abdomen. I squirted for the second time in my life all over his cock.

"Yes, daddy," I cry, lost to the sensations of the most mind-blowing orgasm I've ever experienced.

Niall growls like an animal as I feel his cock explode deep inside of me, filling me with his cum. I take a few moments to realize the words that just came out of my mouth. Shame and shock hit me all at once. The moment I realize what I said, I tense.

Niall is staring at me with even more hunger as he keeps his still hard cock throbbing inside of me. "Is that what you want, baby girl?" he asks, his voice a passionate rasp.

I draw in a deep breath, trying to organize my thoughts. "I'm sorry. I don't know where—"

He growls, cutting me off. "Don't apologize." He wraps his hand around my throat forcefully. "If you want me to be your daddy, I will be. I'll be anything for you, Alicia."

My heart pounds frantically in my chest. I shake my head, sheer embarrassment over slipping up infecting my blood. "I don't know where that came from."

Niall narrows his eyes. "Bullshit, Alicia. You know exactly what you like."

My brow furrows as I search his blue eyes, trying to work out how he would know that. "What do you mean?"

"I know more about you than you think, little lass."

My stomach twists, and I wonder if he knows I am a member of Euphoria in Boston. I haven't been for a few months. In fact, ever since Niall saved me by the river, the thought of fucking another man makes me sick to the stomach. "I'm not sure I want to know what that means."

He smirks. "On your hands and knees for daddy. I'm ready for round two."

I swallow hard before doing as he says. His order only fuels my desire to submit. I've got a feeling tonight is going to be a very long night.

6

## NIALL

*I* wake with Alicia nestled against my chest on the sofa. A pang of longing ignites deep in my gut and my cock is rock-hard against her bare ass. I feel my balls tighten and that blinding desire takes hold of my mind for a moment until I notice the light streaming through the crack in the drapes.

My heart skips a beat as I realize that it's morning, meaning Malachy is back in the house. It leaves me torn, as part of me wants to bury myself inside of her and never leave. Our compromising position in a common area is dangerous, especially since her brother is home.

I grab my cell phone off the floor and check the time. It's six o'clock, luckily. Malachy is rarely up before eight.

"Alicia," I murmur her name softly, placing my hand on her shoulder and rocking her awake.

She mumbles something incoherent, trying to pull away from me.

"We fell asleep, and it's morning," I say, knowing the moment she realizes her brother is back, she'll come to her senses. "Malachy is home."

Her eyes shoot open, and she practically springs off the sofa. "Shit, shit, shit." She rushes around the room, grabbing her strewn clothes from the floor.

I watch her as she frantically pulls them on. "Chill out." I shake my head. "No one has seen us yet."

She stops still and glares at me. "Chill? Malachy is home and we're naked in his fucking movie room."

I watch her as she fastens her bra, hiding her perfect breasts. Internally, I'm recoiling at her ever putting clothes back on. I need our time together to last forever. Alicia pulls on her shirt.

"It's six o'clock in the morning. He won't be up for a couple of hours yet," I point out, to calm her. She's cute when she panics though.

Alicia shakes her head, grabbing her panties.

I clench my jaw, feeling irritated by each piece of clothing she pulls on. The sick, vicious desire pulling at my gut tells me to stop her and fuck her against the wall before she can leave.

Alicia pulls on her jeans, zipping them up. "This never happened." She meets my gaze with a stern look, but I know Alicia like the back of my hand. Even if she's putting a stop to it now, I can see in her eyes she doesn't want to. She walks toward the door, but I chase after her.

I grab her wrist. "It did fucking happen, and it will happen again," I murmur, yanking her hard against me.

Her eyes narrow. "Let go of me, Niall."

I clench my jaw, knowing that is an impossibility. Now I've had her, there's no way I'm ever letting her go. She's mine. *Fuck.* She's been mine for a long damn time. "No chance in hell." I kiss her hard, pouring all of my possessive need into the embrace.

Alicia moans into my mouth as my tongue searches hers. The pent-up desire is still coiling through my veins, even after the line we crossed last night. I need her repeatedly. When we break apart, we're both breathless.

"Remember, baby girl, you're mine now." I grab her hips and hold her tight against me. "I want to hear you say it."

Her eyes find mine, searching for an answer. She knows what I want to hear, but she's unsure about saying it. "I'm yours."

When she doesn't say the word I want to hear, I spank her ass hard. "That's not what I meant, Alicia."

Her throat bobs as she swallows, turning a deep shade of pink. "I'm yours, daddy," she says, her voice instantly turning more innocent. It is enough to drive me insane.

"Good girl," I murmur before kissing her again. "Come to my room tonight at ten o'clock."

Her brow furrows, and I can tell she's considering protesting.

"Malachy will be too damn busy with his virgin to pay any attention to us before you try to make up some half-assed excuse," I say before she can make a case why pursuing this is a bad idea. I know it's a terrible idea, but I don't care. Malachy can kill me if he wants, but Alicia is worth the risk. Damn it, she's worth everything to me.

She worries her bottom lip between her teeth before answering, "Fine, but don't think you can boss me around just because you've fucked me."

I smirk at her as she does not know what she got herself into, letting me fuck her last night. "Oh, little lass, you will learn who is the boss soon enough."

Her emerald eyes flash with irritation, and she yanks her arm free. "You may be a vicious criminal Niall, but you forget that I'm not exactly an angel myself."

I watch after her as she struts confidently out of the room, leaving me with blue balls. We may have fucked four times last night, but it's not enough. Alicia is going to get a wake-up call tonight if she thinks she can talk to me like that.

Alicia is an angel no matter what she says.

I get dressed and head out of the room, walking down the corridor into the entrance hall. My heart stops beating the moment I step toward the stairs, seeing Malachy descend them.

When he sees me, his eyes slowly drop, noticing my clothes—the same clothes I had on yesterday. A smirk plays on his lips. "Dirty dog, been out on the town, aye?"

I try to still my firing nerves, looking my best friend in the eye. "Yes, I went to a friend's place in the city."

His brow furrows. "That's weird. Your car was still here when I got back last night."

I nod. "I took an Uber as I'd been drinking," I say, wishing that I wasn't digging an even bigger hole right now. I've never once had to lie to Malachy so badly in the thirty years I've known him, at least not like this.

He approaches me and pats me on the shoulder. "Good lad, I still think you would benefit from trying out a virgin." He shakes his head. "I bought the most delicious one last night."

I can't deny that my friend is messed up in the head. He's talking about women as if they are fine steaks. "I told you, it's not really my thing, mate." The mere thought of touching any woman other than Alicia irritates me, but that's not something her brother ever needs to know.

"Fair enough." He heads past me. "Get freshened up quickly, as we've got the sit down in the city in an hour. Or did you forget?"

I forgot everything the moment I crossed the line

with his sister. I shake my head. "Of course not, I'll be down in fifteen." I head up the stairs to the top floor where my apartment in his home is, sighing heavily as I shut the door behind me. That was way too close. If I hadn't woken when I did, then we could have been caught red-handed.

I head into the bathroom and get into the shower while it's cold, hoping it will cure the raging hard-on I've been sporting since I woke. It's no use. I grab the base of my cock and tug it hard, shutting my eyes as I remember the four times we fucked last night.

Alicia loves it rough, but she's not seen my rough side yet. I knew I couldn't take it too far, not the first time.

*Fuck.*

*Who am I kidding?*

We can't keep doing this, no matter how badly I want to. Malachy would kill me if he found out I'd defiled his baby sister. He's done terrible things to men that got too close to her. I'm not sure why. Malachy is fucked up. It's as if he can't stop seeing his sister as that vulnerable eight-year-old girl that needs protecting from everyone.

I shake my head, trying to forget about it and focusing on my cock.

Alicia has always been my dirty secret fantasy. She's haunted my dreams for so damn long. I can't believe they finally came true. I shut my eyes and lean back against the wall of the shower, fisting my cock frantically.

Despite how many times I got off last night, I'm still itching for more. It feels like ten o'clock tonight is too far away. I need her now, in this shower with me, moaning as I fuck her against the glass shower screen.

I clench my jaw as I got dangerously close to revealing my true nature. I know too much about my best friend's baby sister. The extent of my obsession with Alicia over the years is bordering on a sickness. I'm not sure she'd be too happy if she knew the stalker-like tendencies I have for her.

It's the reason I could save her from the man down by the river. I followed her that night. Any night she goes out, I follow her. Originally, I'd worried she was heading to Euphoria, a sex club she is a member of. It drives me wild that she goes there, hooking up with random Doms when I'm ready to be everything she wants and more. Luckily for me, she was meeting a friend, and I sat in the bar opposite and watched her in the window seat all night.

My balls draw up as I remember the way it felt to be inside of the woman I've viciously craved for years. When she called me daddy, it felt like my world imploded. Alicia is everything I've needed and more. I want to take care of her. It's all I've ever wanted.

"Fuck," I grunt, feeling my release hit me as I explode. My eyes remain clamped shut as I drain every drop from my balls, wishing my seed was buried deep inside of the woman of my dreams.

Suppressing my sick desire for her over the years has only added fuel to the raging fire. What we have burns too fucking hot, which makes it dangerous.

There is no stopping this, no matter how risky it is. I've tasted her sweet as sin body and been inside heaven on earth. Nothing short of death could stop me now.

I know that could seriously be the outcome of this forbidden love affair if Malachy finds out and flies into one of his savage rages. I've seen it before with Alicia's past love interests; it never ends well. It's testament to how deep my obsession runs with her that I think it's worth risking my life over.

7

## ALICIA

*I* walk down the corridor, adjusting the turtleneck sweater I have on to ensure it hides the mark Niall inflicted on me. The last three nights I've gone to his room, and he makes sure it doesn't heal up, focusing attention on it so that I'm marked as his.

Niall's dominance is beyond arousing. It's titillating to a point I can hardly think of anything but him all day, which is not helpful when I'm studying for my final exam for my PHD.

Malachy has asked me to meet him in his office, which he rarely does. I can't deny that I'm nervous as hell.

*What if he knows about Niall?*

Sasha could have easily heard the two of us getting busy and ratted us out to my brother. It was pretty clear from her obvious flirting that she wanted

Niall. A sickness twists at my gut at the thought of him going near her. I'll clobber her to death if she lays one hand on him. Niall is mine, even though I know it's an impossibility long term. We're off limits to each other, and yet I want him more than I've wanted anything.

I stop outside of Malachy's office door, trying to calm my firing nerves. I bring my clenched fist to the door and knock three times.

"Come in," my brother calls.

I draw in a deep breath and then open the door, plastering on a calm smile despite the storm brewing inside of me. "What's up?" I ask, walking in and flopping down in the seat opposite him.

He smiles. "Can't I just want to see my baby sister?"

I shrug. "Depends what you want."

He laughs and shakes his head. "I haven't seen you for a few days." His brow furrows. "Are you avoiding me because I went to another auction?"

I swallow hard, realizing that the last time we spoke was before the auction. The reason I've avoided him is I'm not sure how to look him in the eye when I've been fucking his best friend and second-in-command.

"No, of course not." I glance down at my entwined fingers. "I just haven't bumped into you. It's your fault for buying such an enormous home."

He sighs. "You have always been such a terrible

liar, Alicia."

I swallow hard, scared that Malachy know about Niall and me. "I'm not lying."

He waves his hand in the air. "Whatever, if you are pissed at me, that's on you." He grabs a piece of paper off his desk and holds it out to me. "This is what I wanted to talk to you about."

My brow furrows as I lean forward in my chair and take the piece of paper from him. It's a legal document and at the top it says *Last will and testament of Malachy McCarthy*. "A will?" I ask.

Malachy nods. "Yeah, with things heating between the Italians and our clan, I thought it best to ensure it was all sorted." He shrugs. "Just in case."

"It's getting that bad?" I ask.

My brother stands and paces the floor. "It's not great, but I don't want you to worry." He stops and meets my gaze. "It's just a precaution. I need you to sign it for me."

I scan over the will, which basically leaves everything to me in the case he remains unmarried and dies. My world would shatter if anything were to happen to him. The mere thought of signing it makes my stomach churn. "Can't you call a truce with the Italians. I can't lose you, Brother." I feel a lump form in my throat.

He walks toward me and places his hands on either side of my shoulders, looking me in the eye. "You have nothing to worry about, little sis. I'll be here to protect you for a long time. It's merely a precaution that Everit brought up at our last meeting."

Everit is the clan's lawyer. A guy that I've met a few times. He gives me the creeps. "I just hate that you're in danger." I run a hand across the back of my neck. "When we left the streets, I thought life would be safer, but it's not." I shake my head. "It's more dangerous."

Malachy smiles wistfully, letting go of my shoulders. "It's safer here in this house. There's nowhere safer in Boston, believe me."

I nod, despite feeling uneasy about this conflict between Malachy's clan and the Italians. It's rare that Malachy tells me anything about the clan's business, so it suggests tensions are worse than ever.

"The will also gives you a share of my company right now, Sis. I think it's time you had some financial independence from me." Malachy's brow furrows. "I'd feel happier if you remain living here, but I know you feel like I keep you captive in this house."

Malachy doesn't keep me captive, but he is overprotective. "There's no way I'm moving out, if that's what you are suggesting."

He smiles. "Good, but I want you to have more freedom." He looks me in the eye. "I'm sorry that I've chased away men from your life in the past. I won't do it next time."

I raise a brow, wondering why he'd bring this up

now. Particularly after what happened between Niall and me. "Not sure there will be a next time. I gave up on that years ago."

There's a wistful look in his eyes. "I'm sorry about that, Alicia." He runs a hand across the back of his neck. "I wanted to protect you from bad men, but maybe I took it too far."

My eyes widen hearing my brother ever admit he did wrong. I don't know what has gotten into him. "It's water under the bridge." I feel uncomfortable discussing this with him, especially since I am lying to him about there being a next time. I should be the one apologizing for fucking his best friend.

"Anyway, will you sign it, please?"

I tilt my head to side. "Hmm, I'll have to think about it."

Malachy rolls his eyes. "Don't be an idiot, Alicia. Sign the damn will."

I smile as my brother is always so easy to wind up. Grabbing the pen from his desk, I sign my name at the bottom of the document. "There, happy now?"

He nods. "Thank you." Mal stands and walks around the desk, setting his hands on my shoulders again. "Are you okay, Alicia?"

I swallow hard, staring into my brother's eyes. "Yes, I'm fine, why do you ask?"

He lets go of my shoulders and shrugs. "No reason, I just don't ask you enough."

My guilt claws at me as I stare into his eyes,

knowing I've betrayed his trust in the worst possible way. "Fair enough." I tilt my head to the side. "Are you okay, big brother?"

His expression hardens. "I'm always okay, you know that, little sis." He runs a hand across the back of his neck. "You can go now. I've got a lot of work to do." He turns his back to me, and I know that's my signal to leave. I have no desire to stay any longer as my guilt is eating at me.

*How can we continue down this path when I feel so bad about it?*

It's clear we have to stop before things get too complicated.

---

I CHECK the corridor as I leave my room, feeling nerves tighten in my stomach. After my conversation with Malachy earlier, I'm on edge. It was convenient timing that he would tell me I should find a man to settle down with after what has happened between Niall and me.

Once I'm confident that there's no one around, I walk toward Niall's room on the other side of the stairs. My heart is pounding with excitement and nerves as I stop in front of his bedroom door, glancing around to ensure no one sees me.

Niall has his own place in the city, but he rarely stays there. It would make more sense for both of us to meet up there, but I think we're both addicted to the thrill. The extra layer of danger that being caught adds to our hot, passionate nights.

I knock on the door and hold my breath, waiting for him to answer.

Niall opens it, wearing nothing but his tight, black boxer briefs. He smiles the most handsome smile at me, making my stomach twist in anticipation. "Evening, little lass," he murmurs, opening the door wide for me to enter.

I step inside, and he shuts the door, walking toward me.

I hold my hands up. "I think we need to stop this."

His brow furrows. "No chance."

"Malachy called me into his office today, and I felt so damn guilty." I shake my head. "How am I supposed to look him in the eye when I'm betraying his trust like this?"

Niall growls softly, a sound that ignites a deep, fundamental need inside of me to be filled with this man. A need that I wish I had the power to resist, but I don't. "You have nothing to feel guilty about, baby girl." He shakes his head. "We're two consenting adults."

I feel my knees wobble beneath me as I stare into his beautiful blue eyes, wishing he didn't hold such power over me. "What if he finds out?"

Niall steps closer, cutting away the distance

between us. "I can't think about that right now, Ali." He lifts his hand to my cheek and caresses it, making my chest ache at the tenderness in his touch.

Pain claws at my chest as I search his eyes, knowing that no matter how much I know we should stop, it's impossible. Niall is under my skin. He's infected my blood, and I can't keep away from him. He lowers his head toward me and presses his forehead to mine. Niall's hand moves from my cheek to the back of my neck, squeezing possessively.

"I ran you a bath, baby girl," he murmurs, making my stomach churn. "Let me wash you."

A tingle ignites between my thighs as I move my head to look him in the eye. "Wash me? I had a shower earlier."

He growls softly. "I don't care. I want to look after my little lass." He moves his hands to my hips and digs his fingertips in. "Now be a good girl and strip for me."

I bite my bottom lip and take a step away from him, untying the bow on the front of my nightdress. It drops to the floor, leaving me naked.

Niall's eyes flash with vicious desire. He makes me feel like the only woman on this earth whenever he looks at me that way. Slowly, his eyes dip down every curve, taking in my naked form. "Perfect," he murmurs, almost to himself. He steps closer and lifts me over his shoulder, taking me by surprise.

"What are you doing?" I ask.

He grunts in response and carries me into his bathroom, which smells of lavender. The room is lit with candles and the huge bath is full, as promised. He sets me down on my feet. "Get in."

I lick my bottom lip, looking at the dominant man I've known all my life. It's crazy to think all this time we've been missing out on something so blissfully perfect. Niall orders me around the way that I've always longed for. "Okay," I say, putting my foot into the balmy water.

Niall grabs my wrist. "Okay, what?"

My heart pounds harder in my chest, making it difficult to think. "Okay, daddy," I say, bringing my other foot into the water and sliding down into the welcoming embrace of the toasty bath. I sigh as the tension eases away the moment I'm immersed in the water. "That feels so good," I murmur.

Niall chuckles softly. "Wait until I get my hands on you," he says, dropping his boxer briefs to the floor.

I watch in awe, admiring every intricate detail of his flawless body. The scar on his right thigh running down past his knee adds to his alluring, bad-boy image that I love so much, coupled with the dark tattoos snaking over his chest and up his neck. The huge, thick length jutting out between his thighs draws my attention in ways nothing else can. It's impossible to contain the soft moan from me. All I want is to feel him stretching and filling me to the hilt.

"Like what you see, baby girl?" he asks.

It's a rhetorical question, as he knows I do. Niall steps into the water by my side. "Move over so I can get behind you," he orders.

I move, allowing him to slide in behind me.

He wraps his powerful arms around my body and holds me against him, groaning softly as his cock presses against my center. "I'm not sure how I'm going to resist fucking you in here," Niall says.

"Then don't resist," I suggest.

He nibbles on the lobe of my ear, making me shudder. The hard press of his cock is hot between my thighs. "First, I'm going to take care of you." He grabs a clean loofah off the side and squirts some sweet-scented body soap onto it before lathering it over my shoulders gently.

I lean back into his warm, comforting embrace. The safety Niall provides is unlike anything I've felt before. There's an unspoken promise that he will take care of me no matter what.

All my life I've been on my own, except for Malachy. I never believed I'd truly find happiness with another human being. Niall gets me the way no other man could.

He's been there through so many things with me, by my side. It's insane that it's taken this long for me to realize the man for me has been living under the same roof for years.

"That feels so good," I murmur, as he moves the loofah lower, lathering my breasts with soap.

Niall's lips press against my shoulder. "Good, I want to make you feel better than you've ever felt before."

I laugh at that. "You already have, many times."

Niall's cock twitches beneath me. "I've barely got started with you, Alicia."

I bite my bottom lip, wondering if that could be true. The sex with him has been out of this world. Surely it can't get any better.

Niall gently lathers the loofah over my abdomen before inching lower over my thighs.

A shudder pulses through me as the need inside of me becomes impossible to bear. I grind my teeth together, trying to stop myself from begging him to touch me.

It's unimaginable, the way he makes me so damn horny. I've always been into sex, but not as much as this. Niall makes it better than anything I've experienced.

"Please," I murmur.

I feel Niall tense beneath me. "Please what, little lass?"

I draw in a deep breath and adjust myself in his lap, letting him feel my center against his cock. "I need you to fuck me."

Niall chuckles. "Not yet, little lass."

I groan as he lets the loofah slide further down my

thighs, away from where I need to feel him.

"Good girls need to learn to be patient," he purrs, lavishing attention on my legs. "I haven't finished cleaning you." He continues to scrub every inch of my body, winding me up with each caress.

When he finally puts the loofah down, I'm breathless and desperate. I groan in frustration as he grabs a bottle of shampoo. "Fuck the hair, I need you." I grab his hand, trying to stop him.

Niall growls, and it's a warning. "Who's the boss, baby girl?"

I can hardly think straight as the yearning for him outweighs everything. "You are, daddy," I say, accepting that Niall is in control. It's the reason I love BDSM. Forcing yourself to submit everything over to another person is the most erotic experience anyone can have. "Do what you want with me."

Niall soaks my hair with the bath water, getting it wet before squirting shampoo into it.

I sigh as he rubs his fingertips through my hair, massaging my scalp as expertly as he does everything else. It makes me wonder if this man is a god. "Damn it, how can you make washing hair so sexual?" I ask.

Niall doesn't answer, instead he continues to focus on me. All of his attention is on taking care of me. Once he's finally finished, he rinses my hair out fully and then wraps a muscular arm around my waist. "You are all clean now, little lass."

I shudder as he presses a kiss to my shoulder, his

cock still hard and throbbing beneath me. All I want is to feel him inside of me. I need that earth-shattering sensation I feel every time our bodies join.

"Please, Niall, I need you," I breathe.

Niall grabs my hips and pushes me forward, allowing him to free his cock. He arrests one of my arms behind my back forcefully, keeping one hand on my hip. "You are going to ride my dick, baby girl."

Excitement coils through my gut and my body trembles with a need so strong it is almost painful. "Yes, daddy," I moan, feeling the tip of his cock nudging at my slick entrance.

I try to force myself over him, but even with me on top I'm utterly at his mercy.

He thrusts his hips upward, burying his cock to the hilt inside of me with one vicious stroke.

The pain of his huge invasion coupled with my hungry desire is inexplicably good. My muscles relax around him as he fucks me roughly.

Water splashes around us as our bodies slip and slide, coming together in frantic movements. All I want is to touch his body, but in this position I can't even see him.

Niall growls as he fucks me harder, the sound beast-like but so arousing. "That's it, take my cock," he pants.

I throw my head back, gripping onto his rock-hard thighs for support. "Fuck, yes," I cry, thankful in that moment that our home is so damn huge and insulated better than a hotel. The thought of trying to be quiet with Niall is almost impossible to imagine.

It feels too amazing to keep quiet. "Can you let me see you, daddy?" I ask, wanting to touch him, kiss him, look into those beautiful crystal blue eyes.

Niall stops still. "Yes, but not in here." He forces me off his cock. "Stand up."

I swallow hard, loving the commanding tone of his voice. I stand and wait for him to issue more orders.

"Out of the bath, baby," he says.

I get out and wait for him, watching the rivulets of water cascading down his god-like body in awe.

Niall gets out and grabs hold of my hips, pulling me against him. Water is dripping from both of our bodies all over the bathroom floor. He grabs my throat hard. "You are so fucking perfect." He kisses me, stealing the little breath I have. Niall releases my throat and then bites my collarbone hard, making me moan. "Hold on to my neck."

I do as he says, wrapping my arms around his neck.

Niall lifts me, placing his arms under my thighs. His cock nudges eagerly at my dripping pussy, ready to fill me.

I search his eyes, feeling the blazing heat of the moment washing over every inch of my body like wildfire.

Niall lowers me onto his cock, still standing, filling

me deeper than ever before.

"Oh fuck," I cry, biting my lip as the pleasure is monumental.

Niall turns feral as his powerful muscles strain to lift me up and down his cock viciously. He growls and captures my lips, pouring every ounce of passion into the kiss. He bites my lip enough to break the skin, licking the blood from it like an animal.

I groan, as it's so fucking sexy. "I'm going to come, daddy" I cry.

He smiles at me. "That's it, baby girl, come on my cock."

My nipples tighten to painful, rubbing against his chiseled chest. I feel the tension release and my body turn limp as my release plows into me with so much force I see stars. My vision blurs, and I feel like I'm floating above my body, watching as Niall continues to fuck me through it.

"I want you to come inside me, daddy," I moan, desperate to feel his cock filling me with his seed.

Niall growls, eyes frantic as his cock feels even harder, larger. He releases, filling my pussy to the brim with cum as it drips down my thighs.

We've waited too damn long to cross the line, and now our attraction has turned into something so deep I feel myself free-falling into a dangerous pit. Our lies and deceit will soon catch up with us. We need to decide whether this is long-term or end it before neither of us can find a way out.

8

## NIALL

*I* stare at my best friend and boss, feeling guilt coil through me. The line I crossed with Alicia a week ago was a direct betrayal of our trust. I've done it every single night since, and I can't stop. It doesn't matter how bad I feel about it, Alicia is my kryptonite.

"Sir, how shall we strike back?" I ask, as Malachy has barely said a word since the meeting started.

He is unfocused as he glances at me. "Find out where they are bringing in their merchandise. I need to cut them off at the source." He cracks his neck, something he only does when he's really irritated. He doesn't seem himself, and I can't help but wonder if he knows something is going on between his sister and me. Although, deep down, I know I'd know about it if he did.

"I've got six guys on this. Do you want me to pull more off other jobs and onto this?" I ask.

Malachy just stares at his desk, as if he didn't hear my question. I clench my jaw, trying to hold together my nerves.

"Sir?" I stare at him, wondering what the fuck has gotten into him today.

He shakes his head. "Sorry, lad. What did you say?"

I can't help the concern pulsing through me. "I said I've got six guys trying to trace the Italian's transport route as we speak. Do you want more resources on this task?"

Malachy rubs a hand across the back of his neck. "We can't pull too many guys off the docks after last night. Six will have to do, but I want them working fucking hard to get me my answers." He cracks his knuckles. "Or else there will be hell to pay."

I nod, hoping that it's only the issues with the Italians that has him so out of sorts. "Agreed. I'll make sure they understand how important it is."

"Good. I think that's everything."

I stand, knowing my cue to leave. Although, I linger. "Is something bothering you, sir?" I frown. "You seem a little…" I'm almost scared to say it as I know how Mal can react when someone asks the wrong question.

"Off?" he asks.

I'm thankful he finishes it for me. "Yeah. Not

meaning any offense by it." Malachy takes offense easily.

He cracks his neck again. "The virgin I bought has been harder work than I expected. That's all."

A flood of relief hits me, and I chuckle. "I'm glad I stayed the fuck away from the auction." He knows nothing about Alicia and me. If he did, this conversation would be different for sure.

Malachy gives me a warning glare. The glare that tells me to back the fuck off. "Normally they are easy to handle, but this girl is different."

I nod. "Well, be careful she doesn't get under your skin. Women can be a nightmare if they get their claws into you."

*I know, since your sister has her claws in me already.*

She always has. The thought is a perilous one, as I'm not sure there could ever be a future for us. "I'll give you an update as soon as we get anywhere with the Italian supply chain issue."

I feel Malachy's eyes on me as I leave the boardroom, shutting the door on him. I rest my back against the hardwood. My heart is hammering frantically. The longer this goes on, the harder it is for me to look Malachy in the eye.

I know we can't continue like this forever, sneaking around behind his back. At the same time, I know there's no chance in hell I'm stopping.

Alicia's half-hearted attempt to put a stop to it five days ago didn't work. She doesn't realize that now I've had her, there is no end to this. I'd die rather than live my life without her in it, a truth so deeply engrained I know it means there is only one way forward.

Malachy will need to know in the end, even if it's too early to play our cards yet. Alicia doesn't know what she wants. Until she does, this has to remain a secret. I've known for a long time that she is my future. I want to spend the rest of my life with her, but I have to convince her to spend hers with me.

Dealing with Malachy is something we can figure out together. There's no other future for me than the one with Alicia by my side. It's the only future I'll accept now that she's part of my life.

I promised Alicia I'd take her out tonight for a proper date, but I know how risky that is.

Malachy isn't stupid, hence why we have to go to the restaurant separately.

We both need to figure this out, and while I know my life won't be complete without Alicia in it, I can't be sure whether she feels the same way.

It will kill me if she doesn't, but I have to respect her wishes. Although, a part of me knows even that isn't an option. The sick stalker inside of me knows that if Alicia tells me no, I won't be able to stop.

I check my watch, noticing it's almost midday and I need to get back to the house to have lunch with my baby girl.

Malachy is rarely at the mansion during the day, so I always go back to eat with her. Or more like eat her. We're both so insatiable we don't have time for food.

I pull out my cell phone and send her a text.

*Running a little late after meeting with Malachy. I'll be over in an hour. What do you prefer, Chinese or Mexican?*

I wait patiently for her reply, hoping she wants Mexican as I've had a hankering for a taco for days now.

*Mexican. Hurry as I'm hungry for you.*

I smirk and shake my head, walking out of the city office block toward my favorite Mexican place around the corner.

There hasn't been a time in my miserable life that I've ever been this happy. Alicia makes me feel like a happy ending is still in the cards for me, something I believed died when I was a child. The moment my father crossed a line he never should have crossed.

I think it's the reason Malachy and I get on so well. We're the same. Although Malachy is lucky that people related to him did not violate him sexually. His father beat him, though, for many years. It took a long time for me to realize that what happened to me as a kid wasn't my fault.

When I ran and ended up on the streets, it was ten times safer for me. I thank the stars every damn day that I found Alicia and Malachy sleeping in the underpass that night. Life would have been very different without them in it.

I head into the little restaurant, feeling my stomach rumble.

Malachy will be angry if we tell him about us, but a part of me hopes he can find it in himself to be happy for us. We've always been like brothers, so why not make it official?

---

The traffic is bad as I head across town, itching to get to Alicia. Finally, I come to the extravagant electric gates of Malachy's mansion, driving up to them. My car is programmed in to be automatically detected by the gate as it swings open, allowing me to drive up the drive.

My heart skips a beat when I see Malachy's Chevy parked in front of the house. It's the same car he drove to the office today, which means he has returned for lunch as well.

*Fuck.*

If he finds out I'm here to bring Alicia Mexican and have lunch with her, it will look suspicious. Malachy never comes back to the mansion in the day, but I have a feeling that his new virgin is the reason. It will only be a problem if he sees me.

The one perk of him having such an enormous house is you rarely see each other, especially if you want to avoid someone. I try to calm my nerves as I park in my spot, turning off the engine.

The scent of the Mexican food makes my stomach rumble as I grab the takeout bag off the seat and head into the house in search of Alicia. Most days I find her sitting in the library, studying for her PHD. I'm in awe of her intelligence and how far she's come considering her lack of education as a child.

I admire her hope to become a doctor. It's a testament to the kind of woman she is, wanting to help people always. It's amazing considering everything we went through as kids, but Alicia has always had the brains.

She was smart before she could afford books or education. It's not a shock that she has the ability to become a doctor. First she got her qualifications as a nurse and now is a trainee doctor, thanks to Alastair's help. The intention is for her to take over from Alastair as a full-time doctor for the clan.

My brow furrows as I walk into the library, finding she's not there. She has been though, as her reading glasses and a book are on the arm of the couch. I turn around and head for the kitchen, but she's not in there either. I set the food down on the counter and try her cell, but it goes to voicemail.

*Fuck's sake.*

The last place I can think to look for her is in her room, so I head upstairs, passing one of the housekeepers Malachy employs.

It irritates me that she lingers too long in the corridor, making it difficult for me to go into Alicia's room. Once she leaves, I head inside to find it empty.

As I'm about to leave the room, I glance out of the window.

That's when I see her, walking across the lawn from the woods. She is wearing a stunning cream dress, and her dark hair is wild and blowing about in the wind. My cock throbs the moment I set eyes on my beautiful, wild Gaelic beauty. She looks utterly magical, walking across the lawn as if she were made to be part of the natural surroundings.

Alicia is a picture of perfection.

The pressing need to be close to her overrules all of my senses as I rush out of the room. Patience isn't something I have when it comes to her. I need to be by her side and can't wait for her to come to me.

I rush down the stairs and head out of the backdoor, marching toward her. The need inside of me tightens, and I know I have to have her here and now. Malachy may be home, but I don't care.

Reason doesn't enter the equation with Alicia McCarthy. I'm insane for her. It's a reckless part of me that may get me killed, but somehow I can't cage it.

The threat of death isn't enough to stop my vicious and insatiable need from determining my actions.

9

## ALICIA

It's a glorious day as I sit perched on the edge of the small pond in the woods, singing in my native language.

One reason I'm so happy is because of Niall. I can't stop smiling ever since we started our affair.

I dip my toes into the cool water below and continue to belt out my song until I notice a woman lingering nearby, watching me. Her presence shocks me, and I jump to my feet. "Who are you?" I ask.

The beautiful girl with fiery red hair swallows, glancing back at the mansion. "My name is Scarlett, and I…" She trails off, and it suddenly dawns on me that's she is the virgin my brother bid on just over one week ago.

The same night that things took a forbidden turn between Niall and me. "Oh no, you're the newest one, aren't you?" I shake my head, wishing he wouldn't buy women the way he does. "My brother can be such a fucking pig."

Scarlett's eyes widen. "Brother?"

I nod and close the distance between us. "Yeah, Alicia McCarthy. It's nice to meet you, Scarlett." I hold my hand out to her.

She shakes it. "It's nice to meet you." She glances at the mansion anxiously again. "I'm not supposed to be outside, but I was going crazy stuck in that room."

I laugh. "Don't worry. I won't tell him. My brother is amazing to me, but I know how trying he can be with most people." I glance at her arms and neck, surprised there aren't any bruises or cuts like normal. "You don't look as beaten up as most of the girls." I know my brother is sick because of the things he does to those poor virgins, but I know that he's disturbed by his past. I walk back to my spot by the lake and dip my feet back in. "Why don't you sit with me a while?"

Scarlett smiles. "That would be nice." She sits next to me. "You have a beautiful singing voice, by the way. What song were you singing?"

"Óró Sé do Bheatha 'Bhaile," I say. "It's a Gaelic song. In English, the title is Oh, Welcome Home." I smile as I remember the times on the streets when Malachy and I would sing together. "You may not believe this, but Malachy has a beautiful singing voice too. Better than mine, even." I laugh. "Not that he ever uses it. He prefers to fight rather than sing."

"You stayed true to your roots then, learning Gaelic?" Scarlett asks.

I nod, feeling a tightness pull at my chest. "Yes, my mother taught me when I was little. Before she died." I notice the pity in her eyes as she looks at me.

"Sorry to hear that. It must have been rough for you and Malachy."

I realize at that moment this girl knows nothing about my brother. "Malachy loved my mother, but we are half-siblings." I sigh heavily. "I think it was easier for him once our father was gone. He abused Malachy from a young age."

"What did he do to him?" She asks.

I know Malachy hates me telling people about his past. "Malachy's mother died in childbirth, and our father blamed him for it. He beat him from a very young age." I shake my head. "I shouldn't tell you all this. He would kill me if he knew."

"Don't worry. I've got no intention of telling."

I smile at her, as she's not like the other women he's purchased before. They were normally stuck-up, materialistic women who were in it for the money. "Thanks. I wish Malachy would stop buying women at those disgusting auctions." I glance at her. "No offense."

"None taken."

I hum the song I'd been singing as a comfortable atmosphere surrounds us. After a few minutes, I break the silence. "Can I be rude and ask why you auctioned yourself off like that?" I can't help but feel curious about why such a nice girl sold her virginity to man like my brother "You're not like the others."

"I had no other option. My mom is sick." Her brow furrows. "In what way am I different from the others?"

I clap my hands. "That explains it. All the women Malachy has purchased up to now are in it for a fancy car or nice clothes. They weren't doing it for a worthy cause." I let out a heavy breath. "I wish Malachy would settle down with a nice girl like you." I mean that more than she can know. One question has been on the tip of my tongue ever since she sat down, but I'm almost scared to learn the truth about my sick and twisted brother. "Is he mistreating you?" I look Scarlett in the eye.

She doesn't answer right away, as if contemplating the question. "Not yet." Her throat bobs as she swallows.

"What the fuck is going on here?" Malachy's voice cuts through the clearing.

I laugh and jump to my feet, despite knowing how pissed he's going to be that we were hanging out. "Malachy, I was getting to know your newest purchase. She seems nice." I walk toward my brother and pull him into a hug, although he's as tense as stone.

When I break free, Malachy's eyes are full of rage and fixed on his virgin. "How the fuck did you get out of the room?" he asks, his eyes fixed on Scarlett with dangerous intensity. He doesn't even acknowledge me.

Scarlett gets up and faces him. "A housekeeper came in and asked if I could give her some time while she was cleaning." She shrugs. "I assumed it was fine to get some fresh air since I've been cooped up in that room for a week now."

Malachy still doesn't look at me. "Alicia. Leave us."

"Brother, you need to chill out. Scarlett wasn't doing—"

"Alicia. I said, leave us. Don't make me ask a third time," he growls.

I feel bad about leaving the poor girl to the wrath of my brother, but I won't disobey him. I shoot her an apologetic look before leaving her with my beast of a brother. The man is bordering on feral.

I rush out of the forest and make my way across the lush lawns toward the mansion. One glance backward tells me they are still in the forest together. I pity the poor, defenseless girl that Malachy has at his mercy.

I glance forward again and stop moving when I see Niall stalking into the garden with his eyes fixed on me, his hard muscles bunched and tense as he prowls toward me.

The dark, dirty desire pulsing to life in his ice-blue depths is enough to set me ablaze. Niall can't lose control out here, not while Malachy is home and in the garden, nonetheless. I hasten my steps toward him. "Hey, Niall—"

He collides with me, pulling me against his lips in one hard jerk. I hold on to his arms, trying to steady myself as his tongue plunders into my mouth hungrily. There's no quenching his ravenous hunger or mine. The moment we crossed the line between friends and lovers, all hell broke loose.

I force him away from me with all the strength I can muster, panting for oxygen. "Not here. Malachy is in the woods with his virgin."

The mention of Malachy is enough to snap him out of it. "Fine. Your room, now," he orders, gently resting his hands on my hips. "I can't wait any longer."

I chuckle softly. "Well, maybe you will have to wait."

Niall growls like an animal and tightens his grip on my hips. "Don't make me fuck you out here in the open where your brother can hear."

My stomach tightens at the viciousness in his voice. I don't doubt that he has that little control over his urges. A part of me wants him to pull me around the side of the building and fuck me against the wall. "I've got work to do," I say, remembering that Alistair is expecting me to help with some medical research this afternoon.

Niall lifts me off the ground, making me yelp in

surprise. "Wrong answer, little lass," he rumbles, carrying me around the corner. He drops me to my feet and presses me against the wall of the mansion. "On your knees."

My eyes widen at the order. "Not here, Niall. What if we get—"

"Now," he rumbles, lacing his fingers tightly in my hair.

I sink to my knees in front of him, feeling a mix of shame and lust warring with each other. My desire for this man is unwavering.

Niall unzips his pants and frees his hard, thick length from them. His cock bobs in front of my lips, dripping with precum.

I lick my lips as the hunger for him rises inside of me like a tidal wave.

The moment I reach for him, Niall grabs my hands to stop me. "Open wide." His dominant and cold gaze stills my heart as I open my lips for him, submitting in the way I always crave.

Niall rams his hard cock to the back of my throat with one thrust. I gag and reach out for his thighs, only for him to swat my hands away and grab the back of my neck. "Take it, baby girl. Every damn inch," he growls softly, making my nipples harden.

I struggle to breathe through my nose, relaxing my throat as he assaults it. Niall is viciously dominant, and it's so arousing. At thirty-eight years old, I've grown pretty confident of my tastes in sex. Although

I've never found a man to settle down with, I've always known that I'm a submissive and have had sexual relationships with Doms. Niall is clearly a Dom, which makes this more perfect than I ever expected.

He also likes me calling him daddy, an aspect of the BDSM world I've always been curious about but never explored.

I choke on his cock as he holds it down my throat, coming undone and spilling every drop from his balls down it.

When he finally frees me, I gasp for air. "Are you trying to kill me?"

He laughs. "Oh, come on, little lass. You know you love it." He yanks me to my feet and lifts me against the wall, surprising me.

"What are you doing?" I ask.

He smirks. "Fucking you, what does it look like?"

"You already came," I point out.

He chuckles and drags the head of his still hard cock through the center of my panties. "I'm ready to come again, baby girl."

I rest my head against the wall and moan. "Fuck me, daddy," I murmur.

He smirks at me. "You don't need to ask me twice."

Niall's powerful arms hold me against the wall as he uses one hand to force my panties aside. A hot, tense moment passes between us as his cock throbs against my center and his gaze burns a mark on my soul. He pushes through my entrance and fills me completely, knocking the air from my lungs.

We shouldn't be doing this at all, let alone out here when my brother is in the woods a few hundred yards away.

"Fuck," I whisper, biting my lip to stop myself from screaming. The danger we're flirting with is ludicrous, but it makes the experience all the more intoxicating.

"That's it, little lass, take my cock," he grunts, thrusting his hips brutally and rapidly. He takes me without mercy and without a care in the world.

The rough brickwork grazes my skin, but the pain is welcome as he drives in and out of me like a wild animal. I claw my fingers into his solid shoulders, using him to ground me.

Niall sucks at the mark at my neck, making the ache between my thighs heighten. Our breathing is frantic and out of sync as he drives us both toward the cliff's edge. No man has had such masterful skill over my orgasms in my life. Niall knows how to take me along for the ride, rather than leaving me behind.

It's difficult to believe that we've been missing out on this all these years. "Oh my God, yes, daddy," I murmur, biting his shoulder to stop myself from screaming out.

Blazing pleasure sweeps through my body as he sends me over the edge, free falling as the release washes over me. I meld my lips to his, knowing it's the only way to stop myself from screaming at the top of my lungs.

Niall grunts as he comes undone too, releasing deep inside of me. Our bodies continue to rock together long after we've both released, as if neither of us can bear the thought of leaving the warmth of each other.

I don't know how long we remain fixed in that position, clawing onto each other as if our lives depend on it. His lips tease over mine, kissing me tenderly.

"Scarlett, wait," Malachy shouts across the other side of the mansion, making both of us tense.

"Shit," I murmur against his lips, trying to push Niall's huge size off of me.

Niall lets me down and I slide my panties back into place. He shoves his cock back into his pants. "You go left, I'll go right. Meet in the kitchen," he whispers softly before stealing another kiss.

My heart is pounding frantically as he slips away, leaving me to head toward Malachy's voice. I turn around the corner in time to see Scarlett rush past me, looking rather shaken.

Malachy chases after her.

"What's going on?" I ask.

Malachy barely looks my way. "Nothing, keep out of it, Sis." He marches past me without stopping, to my relief.

This girl of his is distracting him from the fact I'm fucking his best friend.

I head into the mansion just in time to see Malachy disappear upstairs after his woman. There's something different about this girl. I can only hope that Malachy sees it and finally breaks the cycle he's been trapped in.

She's nicer than any of the gold diggers he's purchased before. I could see them both together for sure.

Niall is in the kitchen, heating the Mexican food he bought. "That was too fucking close," I say quietly, making him turn around.

He nods. "Tell me about it."

An awkward, heavy silence settles between us as he continues to busy himself with the food. We both know we're playing with fire. It's the reason for the tension.

Neither of us wants to say what we're both thinking. This has to stop before it gets out of hand.

## 10

## NIALL

Anger builds inside of me, as it's been two days since Malachy almost stumbled on us in a compromising position. Alicia called off our dinner date, spooked by the close call. I didn't realize at the time that was her calling us off completely.

Alicia has avoided me ever since, and it's driving me crazy. She won't return my texts or calls, and she's locked me out of her room.

We crossed a line we shouldn't have crossed, that is true, but now that we have, I can't let go. Alicia is my world, and I won't have her take the only shred of good from my life of darkness.

Normally I'm not home in the morning as Malachy has me run errands, but today I've given them to Rory to handle. It means I'll be able to ambush her and force her into seeing that she's wrong.

We are made for each other.

I enter the house quietly and head down the corridor toward the library, where the door is cracked open. Alicia sits hunched over a book on the table, scribbling something down on a piece of paper next to it. My heart pounds frantically in my chest as I inch the door open further.

The creak alerts her of my presence and her emerald eyes find mine in an instant.

"What are you doing here?" she asks.

I step inside and shut the door, turning the lock. "You gave me no other choice, little lass."

Her eyes flash with irritation as she stands, folding her arms over her chest. "Get out."

I shake my head. "Since when do you give the orders?"

Alicia steps around the table, putting it between us. "We got too reckless. You know it. I know it. There's nothing to discuss. It's over, Niall."

I walk toward her, feeling that dangerous rage building below the surface. She doesn't know what the fuck she's talking about.

"Don't come any closer," she orders, holding her arms out in front of her.

I keep moving, grabbing the table and pushing it out of the way. "If you think you can walk away from me like that, you underestimated the type of man I am, Ali."

Alicia takes a step back to each of mine until she hits the bookcase behind her. "Niall, what are you—"

"Don't speak, baby girl." I feel the grip on my control slipping as my rage builds. "I know everything about you because I've wanted you for so damn long," I say, stopping with a foot between us. "You don't get to rip that away from me now I've finally had a taste. No chance."

Her brow furrows. "What do you mean you know everything about me?"

I tilt my head to the side. "I know you sing when you are sad and lonely, trying to drown your sorrows in music. I know you take your coffee black. Your favorite coffee place is Straza on the corner of Traveler Street. I know you crave a dominant man, hence why you attend Euphoria."

Her eyes widen. "How could you know about that?" She shakes her head. "Have you been following me?"

I close the gap between us. "I know that your favorite food is Mexican. You always order quesadillas at The Three Amigos." I reach for her cheek and cup it in my hand, gently brushing a hair away from her face. "I know everything about you, and I also know that you want me as badly as I want you."

Alicia yanks my hand away and rushes out of my grasp. "Niall, what the hell? Is that how you came to my aid so quickly down by the river? You follow me everywhere?" She shakes her head, searching my eyes in hope I will deny it.

"Yes," I say simply, closing the gap between us again. "I've wanted you for too long, little lass. Now I've had you, I have no intention of letting you go."

"You are certifiably insane. Who stalks a girl they live with?"

I close her in against the bookshelf again, pressing my hands on either side of her to ensure she can't run. "You can call it stalking if you want. I know you feel it too."

She licks her bottom lip, her eyes darting from side to side as she tries to plan her escape from me. There is no escape. "Niall, please let me go."

I grab hold of her throat and force her to look me in the eye. "You don't want that, not really." I force my lips against hers, probing my tongue through her unwilling lips.

Alicia tries to fight, but I grip hold of her. Slowly, her reluctance melts away and her tongue dances with mine as the fire of our passion rekindles to an inferno.

When we break apart, she's breathless and flushed. The look in her eyes is uncertain as she shakes her head. "You have issues."

I shrug. "I always have had issues, and you knew that when you jumped in bed with me." I tighten my grip on her hips and force her toward the desk. "Now,

I'm going to punish my naughty girl for ignoring me for two days."

Alicia shudders as I force her face first over the desk, lifting her skirt to reveal her perfect ass visible in the black thong she's wearing.

I spank her right cheek hard, making her squeal.

"Niall, what are you—"

I spank her left cheek equally hard. "You know that's not the name I want to hear, little lass."

Her thighs tremble as I spank her right cheek again before moving to the left, giving equal attention to each cheek.

"Fuck, daddy, stop," she cries, making my cock leak into my tight boxer briefs.

"That's more like it, baby girl." I lean over her back and bite the lobe of her ear softly. "Daddy will not stop, because you need to be punished."

I sit down on the chair and pull her over my lap, giving me better access to every part of her body.

Alicia tenses as I run a finger through her soaking wet cunt, groaning at how wet she is.

"It looks like you enjoy being punished. Open your mouth," I order.

Alicia hesitates before opening her mouth.

I slide my finger coated in her juices into it. "Taste yourself for me, baby."

Alicia moans as she closes her mouth around my finger and sucks it clean.

"Good girl," I purr, loving the way she squirms over my lap.

My cock is hard and throbbing against her lower abdomen. "You've been such a naughty girl." I tear her panties off of her and part her ass cheeks, spitting onto her tight little asshole. I slide my finger back into her cunt, getting it suitably wet before probing at her little back hole.

Alicia gasps as I gently add pressure. "What are you—"

Her question earns her a hard spank. "No questions. I'm in charge."

She relaxes a little as I continue to add pressure to her hole, easing my finger in there slowly.

I spit on it again, getting it suitably wet to allow my finger inside.

Her tight hole finally allows me inside. Alicia's deep moan derails me as I finger fuck her ass. "Do you like that?" I ask, moving my finger faster.

"Yes, daddy," she replies, her voice laced with ardent desire.

I smirk as I continue to finger fuck her, spanking her with my other hand.

"Oh God," she cries.

I stop as I can feel her muscles contract, warning me she's about to climax. "No chance, naughty girls don't get to come so easily." I pull my finger from her ass and lift her off of me. "On your knees."

Alicia searches my eyes before dropping to her

knees like the good little submissive she is. My little submissive.

"Take it out," I order.

She licks her lips before unzipping my pants and freeing my rock-hard cock from the confines of my pants. Alicia strokes it up and down with her dainty fingers.

"Suck it, baby girl."

Alicia doesn't have to be asked twice. All her reluctance has melted away and her eyes are overcome with a passionate desire that mimics mine. She opens her mouth and slips my cock right to the back of her throat, making me grunt.

I lace my fingers in her hair, knowing without a doubt that this is heaven.

My hips meet her actions as I thrust my cock into the back of her throat, fucking it as my hand keeps control of her speed. I love having total control over her body, but what I love more is the way she so easily gives me it. Alicia trusts me more than any girl I've ever been with, and it makes the sex better than anything I've experienced before.

"Fuck, your throat is amazing," I growl, lacing my fingers tighter in her hair and increasing the speed of my strokes.

Alicia's fingernails dig into my thighs as I force her to choke on my cock. Saliva spills down her chin and onto my shaft. Tears prickle at her eyes as she struggles to breathe.

Never have I seen such a beautiful sight in my life. Alicia with my cock thrust into her throat and saliva spilling everywhere is a piece of artwork.

She's a picture of perfection.

My balls tighten and I release her hair, knowing that this can't be over yet. I need to be inside of her.

"Stand," I order.

Alicia's eyes flash with annoyance, but she does as I say. "Just so you know, I haven't forgotten that you are a crazy stalker."

I laugh at that. "No, but you don't mind having my cock all the way down your throat, do you?"

Her eyes narrow. "You are one cocky son of a bitch."

I stand and grab her hips forcefully, dragging her against me. "That's no way to speak to me, is it?" I grab her throat, squeezing. "Don't make me rinse your dirty little mouth out with soap."

Alicia trembles as I bring my lips to the mark between her collarbone and neck. The mark I made on her the first time we fucked. Gently, I suck the tender flesh, knowing I never want it to disappear from her body.

I want her to look in the mirror and see it and think of me. I want her to know that I own her in every single sense of the word.

"Lie on your back on the desk," I order.

Alicia raises a brow but doesn't question me.

I watch as she lies down, parting her thighs for me

so I can see that perfect little cunt nestled between her creamy, thick thighs. "Play with yourself for me, baby girl."

Her eyes flash, and she slides a finger down between her thighs, stroking the sensitive spot. My cock throbs as I watch her obey me, touching herself frantically as she drives toward the pleasure I denied her.

Alicia's cheeks deepen in color as she pants, closing in on that orgasm she so longs for.

"Stop," I order.

She whines, shaking her head. "Please, I'm so close."

"Exactly, that's why you have to stop." I close the gap between us and grab hold of her hand, forcing it away from her pussy. I lightly spank her pussy, which results in a strangled moan.

"Fuck, I need to come," she cries. "Please, daddy, please let me come."

I shake my head and stand between her wide thighs, rubbing the head of my cock through her center. I tease her with the head, stroking it up and down her dripping wet entrance. "I'm not sure I've punished you enough yet, baby girl."

My cock longs to be wrapped in her heat, but I know I can't give her that. She ignored me for two fucking days, so she needs to learn what happens to girls that disobey. She needs to suffer the way I suffered.

I tighten my grip around my cock and jerk off.

Alicia's brow furrows. "What are you doing? Fuck me,"

I shake my head. "No, little lass. I'm going to come in your pretty little pussy and leave you gagging for more." I continue to fist my cock up and down, driving myself closer to release.

Alicia stares up at me in shock. "I'll just make myself come without you then." Her hand slides between her thighs, and I grab hold of it with my free hand.

"No chance. This is your punishment. You will not come until I give you permission."

"Psycho," she pants, breathless, as her chest heaves up and down in her tight, black shirt.

I continue to get myself off, driving myself to the edge. "Fuck, I'm going to come in that pretty little pussy of yours," I growl as my release barrels into me hard. The first spurt of creamy cum flies from my cock onto her pussy before I thrust inside of her, coating her insides with my seed.

Alicia's eyes dilate as she takes the single thrust of my cock, allowing me to fill her. She licks her lips like the hungry whore she is.

It's tempting to remain buried inside of her forever, but once I've drained ever drop, I slip my cock back into my pants. I pull Alicia's skirt down over the mess I made and grab her panties, slipping them over her legs and putting them in place. "I want you to stay like that the rest of the day. If you come, I'll know and your punishment will be far worse." I yank her to her feet and angle her face up. "See you at my room, ten o'clock. Don't dare clean yourself up or touch yourself."

Alicia's eyes widen. "I'm too damn horny, Niall."

I grab a fistful of her hair, hard. "You should have thought about that before you ignored me," I growl, before letting go and walking away.

Alicia will need to learn that there is no getting out of this. Now I've had her, I'm never letting her go. The quicker she can accept that, the better it will be for both of us.

## 11

## ALICIA

Today has been the longest day of my life.

I'm so horny it's intolerable, and yet the submissive side of me won't allow me to succumb to my cravings.

Niall is mental, but I think it's part of what I like about him. He stalked me for God knows how long, a fact that should turn me off, and yet I've been struggling to think about anything but sex since he left this morning.

My clit is practically throbbing for me to touch it, but I won't.

Instead, I try and fail to ignore the sensations overtaking my body ever since Niall touched me. His cum hasn't been washed away, but slowly seeped out into the biggest pair of panties I own.

I feel so damn dirty, but in a good way.

I glance at the clock, noticing it's only nine

o'clock. One hour until I'm supposed to go to his room, but I don't think I can wait any longer.

Niall might not be happy if I disobey his direct order, but I need him right now. I stand from my bed and head out of my room, crossing the hallway to his door.

My heart is pounding so hard I can hear it as I knock on his door.

His footsteps on the other side tighten the excitement inside of me. Niall opens the door and raises a brow. "It's not ten o'clock yet."

I force the door open and walk past him into his room. "I couldn't wait. I'm going fucking crazy."

He shuts the door and locks it. "Is that right, but you know coming here early directly violates my order."

"Come on, Niall. I've waited so long."

He tilts his head, observing me with an irritating amusement. "Now I'm going to tease you for an hour until you're so desperate you are crying for me to make you come."

*Oh shit.*

Maybe it was a mistake coming here early. I shake my head. "No, I can't stand anymore torture."

Niall chuckles. "Believe me, baby girl, torture doesn't feel as good as the way I make you feel." He steps toward me, closing the gap between us. "Now strip."

I tremble at his command, feeling utterly spent

and used before he's even started with me. Slowly, I unbutton my shirt, teasing him the only way I can.

Niall loses his patience, growling like the insatiable beast he is. He grabs hold of my hips and yanks the rest of the buttons apart, breaking them off.

I gasp at the look in his eyes. A look that makes me feel more valued than I've ever felt in my thirty-eight years of life.

"You're too fucking slow, little lass." He unhooks the fastening on my bra, dropping it to the ground.

My nipples are hard, longing to feel his mouth on them.

Niall groans and captures one between his lips before tugging it gently between his teeth in a way that sends seismic waves through my entire body. "I can never get enough of this," he murmurs before doing the same to the other.

I lace my fingers in his hair, letting my head fall back as he drives me wild with his touch, his mouth. Everything about him calls to me in the most primitive way.

He unfastens my skirt and drops it to the floor. "Alicia, you better not have cleaned up. Why have you changed your panties?"

I raise a brow. "First reason, you tore my other panties. Second, I put these on because they'd keep your cum inside of me better."

Niall growls and devours my mouth in a frenzy, demanding my submission as he drives his tongue around mine. When he breaks away, he looks otherworldly. "Panties off now so I can fill you back up."

I feel lightheaded as I pull my panties down, resisting the urge to rub myself. I've never been so needy in my entire life.

Niall drops to his knees in front of me and sucks my clit into his mouth, making my legs buckle as I grab hold of his muscular shoulders for support.

"Oh my God," I cry, struggling to draw air into my lungs as he works his tongue around my clit. The need for release is so intense I can hardly think straight.

Niall stops. "God has nothing to do with it, little lass." His crystal blue eyes flash with mischief.

"Sorry, daddy," I say, wanting nothing more than to feel his mouth back on my pussy.

"Good girl," Niall purrs.

It's so satisfying hearing him call me that. All I want to do is to please him, no matter how messed up he is. It is a little creepy that he stalks me around the city, but it makes me feel desired. We're both messed up. Victims of our lack of childhood, but his childhood was far worse than mine.

Niall sucks my clit, and all thoughts disappear. I moan as he drives me toward the cliff's edge with his tongue, pushing me nearer to the one thing I've been craving for hours.

My thighs shudder as I feel my release closing in on me.

Then he stops, leaving me panting and frustrated. "No, please don't stop. I need to come," I whine.

Niall glances at his watch. "Sorry, baby girl, it's only quarter past nine."

I groan and stomp away from him, heading toward the bathroom.

"Where the fuck are you going?" he asks.

I glance over my shoulder. "I'm going to take matters into my own hands."

Niall moves so fast I can't beat him as I dash for the bathroom, trying to shut the door in his face. "Over my dead body," he growls, forcing the door open and grabbing hold of me. He hoists me over his shoulder and carries me back into his room. "You've left me with no choice," he mutters, putting me on the bed and fastening shackles around my wrists and ankles.

"Niall, this is not fair," I complain.

He smiles at me, running his hand gently down my cheek. "It's what happens when you are disobedient, Alicia." Niall walks toward his closet, leaving me fighting against the restraints.

When he returns, he's holding three implements. A ball gag, spreader bar, and nipple clamps. The mere thought of those on my nipples makes them ache. I've never tried them before, even in my time attending Euphoria. "Now it's time to show you what real pleasure can feel like."

"Niall, what about a safe word?" I shake my head. "I can't say anything with the gag in my mouth."

Niall nods. "Click your fingers twice if it gets to be too much."

He attaches the spreader bar first, linking it to the chains around my ankles. Next, he adds the clamps to my nipples, which are light and not as painful as I expected. Finally, he pushes the ball gag in my mouth and fastens it around the back of my head.

"Now you are entirely at my mercy with nowhere to escape to." He rubs his fingers in a circular motion on my clit, setting me on fire. "Exactly how I like it."

Niall opens the drawer in the nightstand and pulls out a small vibrator, turning it on. "Time to show you how good delayed gratification can be." There's an evil, sadistic glint in his eyes. One that tells me this is going to be pure erotic torture. My stomach twists with both nerves and excitement.

I swallow hard, waiting for the pleasurable agony to begin.

Niall draws it out, pressing the vibrator onto the inside of my thigh and gently bringing it closer to my pussy, only to move it at the last moment.

I grunt in frustration, hating the way he denies me what I want.

No Dom has ever put me through this much delay for pleasure before, and it's downright irritating.

Niall grazes the vibrator over my clit, making my hips jolt upward. It feels like an electric shock. An intense, pleasurable sensation that surpasses anything I've felt before.

*Fuck.*

I hold his gaze as he smiles at me with that knowing smile.

"Feels good, aye?" he asks.

I nod, struggling to draw breath into my lungs.

*Keep going, please.*

I hate being unable to beg with this damn gag in my mouth, but it gives Niall an ultimate power over me. It gives him a trust I've given no man before.

He moves to my other thigh, slowly drawing closer to where I need to feel the pleasure. He grazes it gently over my clit again, turning me into a molten puddle as he moves it between my entrance and clit over and over.

My eyes roll back in my head as he takes me somewhere I've never been before. Heaven, perhaps. It feels like I'm floating on air as he drives me closer to my orgasm.

I bite my cheek, trying to stop myself from crying out. The last thing I want is for him to stop this now. It's no use though. My body betrays me, and he turns off the toy.

"Don't think that not moaning is going to fool me, baby girl. You won't come until my cock is deep inside of you."

I rest my head back against the pillow, surrendering to the fact I have zero control in this situation.

I can't speak, can't move. Niall has access to every single part of my body, and I have no way of stopping him. The clamps on my nipples are beyond arousing. They send torturous pleasure through me.

The zip of his trousers coming down is the best sound I've heard all damn day. He strokes his straining cock in his hand before rubbing it through my soaking wet juices.

I'm a trembling shadow of the woman I once was with nothing on my mind other than my climax and Niall's cock.

He pushes forward, sliding every inch into me with one thrust. Niall kisses me softly, holding still inside of me as my body screams for everything he has to give me. "You are so damn perfect," he murmurs before sucking on the sensitive spot where he marked me our first night together. The past two days away from him have dulled the bruising.

The dull ache of the bruise adds to the insurmountable buzz I feel with his cock stretching me, finally.

Niall moves in and out of me, slowly at first. We hold each other's gaze and I feel the buildup begin faster than it ever has before. As I stare into this man's eyes, I have never been more certain that we were made for each other than in this moment.

The ferocity in his gaze increases with each stroke as his muscles tense. The beast inside of him is longing to break free as he fucks me rougher. I love it.

## VICIOUS DADDY

The sensation of being taken by him so viciously is addictive.

Niall bites my collarbone hard enough to break through the skin. The pain is unbelievably good. "I own you, Ali. Every fucking part of you." His eyes are frantic as his pace increases. "You will never have another man inside of you so long as I still have breath in my lungs and a heartbeat in my chest."

He grabs hold of my hips hard enough to bruise as he loses control. Our bodies meld together in a passionate clash of skin against skin as he fucks me like a wild beast. The rush of pleasure tightens around me as I feel the orgasm I've been waiting for crash into me.

A flood of hot liquid squirts from my pussy, gushing all over Niall's cock as the most heavenly orgasm washes over me. I cry and scream into the ball gag, feeling wave after wave of pure ecstasy infiltrate my blood.

Niall's eyes hold mine as I experience a world-altering sensation. Every nerve ending in my body sizzles with explosive heat. For a moment, I'm pretty sure I lose consciousness as my mind blanks out.

Niall's growl brings me back to the present. His muscles strain above me as he pumps two more times before releasing every drop of his cum inside of me.

The image of him panting and straining over me is beautiful. All I want to do is touch every inch of his powerful body, but I can't.

Niall's eyes find mine, and he reaches around the back of my head to unfasten the ball gag. Quickly, his tongue replaces the gag before I can say a word.

I feel myself drowning in our intimacy, certain that there's no chance in hell I'm ever going to be happy without this man in my life.

A dangerous notion, but one I can't shake.

## 12

## NIALL

Alicia's head rests on my chest when I wake in the early hours of the morning.

We had the most intimate sex we've shared yet. If anything, the fact she knows how obsessed I am with her made her even more desperate for me.

I shift my arm from under her and glance at the clock. It's only four o'clock in the morning.

I scrub my hand over my face before swinging my legs out of the bed.

My hunger for the woman sleeping in my bed is impossible. It doesn't matter how many times I have her; the need grows with each kiss and caress.

The desire is unquenchable. My cock is hard right now, straining in my briefs as if it has a mind of its own.

I need to relieve myself, and I'm not entirely sure Alicia would appreciate me fucking her in her sleep.

Clenching my fists, I force the idea out of my head. I'm sick enough to do it, to wake her with my cock stretching her tight little cunt.

Part of me is sure she'd love it, but the last thing I want to do is scare her away.

Instead, I get up and head into the bathroom. My cock is leaking into the fabric, so I free it and stroke it up and down, picturing the beauty in the other room.

As I try to get myself off, the sick and twisted part of me that longs to be inside of her while she sleeps grows. I walk to the cracked open door and watch her as she sleeps, fisting myself ferociously.

"Fuck it," I murmur under my breath, walking back into the bedroom. I chuck my boxer briefs on the floor and get back under the covers, my cock straining so hard.

I gently pry the covers from her body, groaning when I see her pussy. She's sleeping on her back with her legs parted, giving me a perfect show. I gently run my finger through her pussy, feeling how wet she is already.

The last thing I should do is shove my cock in her right away, but the thought of her waking with me inside her drives me crazy. I can't control myself any longer as I position myself over her and slide every inch through her wet entrance.

Alicia tenses, eyes opening wide at the sudden invasion. "Niall, what are you—"

I kiss her, silencing the question. "I need you so

fucking bad, baby girl," I whisper against her lips, thrusting my cock in and out of her tight heat.

She moans against my mouth, bringing her hands to my hair and running her fingers through it. "Fuck, it feels so good," she murmurs.

I rest my cock deep inside of her, grinding in circles so that I stimulate her clit at the same time.

Alicia's eyes flash as she moans deeply, her cheeks flushing a deep red as I push her toward her climax.

The need to make her feel better than she's ever felt before drives me insane. I need her to tell me I'm the only man who has ever made her feel this good.

"How does it feel, little lass?" I ask.

She shakes her head. "So fucking good. Don't stop," she rasps, clawing onto my arms desperately.

"Never," I murmur, continuing to grind in circles rather than thrusting. It's an oddly intimate sensation, feeling so interconnected with the woman beneath me.

Alicia's breathing deepens as she gets closer to orgasm. "I'm going to come, daddy," she warns, rubbing her hands down my chest. "Make me come," she cries.

"Fuck, baby girl," I grunt, quickening my pace as I push her closer to the edge.

I feel it the moment she comes undone, the squirt of juice flooding around my cock and her muscles spasming as pleasure racks her body. "You are such a good girl, squirting on my cock like that," I growl, kissing her frantically. "Now, I'm going to fuck you hard."

Alicia whines as I pull my slick cock from her cunt, forcing her onto all fours in front of me. "Yes, daddy, give it to me hard."

I slide my cock into her, grabbing hold of her hips with such force I know I'll leave bruises.

Alicia arches her back, willing me to take everything. Her tight little asshole looks perfect in this position and the thought of fucking it turns me feral. I lose control, slamming into her so hard it's as if I'm trying to break her in two.

There's no way I can rein it in as I take what I want from her. My mind turns blank and the only word beating through it like a drum is *mine*.

Alicia moans so loudly, which only encourages my rough treatment of her.

I grab hold of a fistful of her hair and yank it toward me, forcing her to arch her back upwards. "That's it, take my cock," I growl.

Alicia doesn't tense or recoil against me, trusting me entirely with her body. It's such a satisfying sensation knowing that she trusts me so fully.

I let go of her hair and grab her throat instead, applying the perfect amount of pressure.

Alicia groans as I feel her pussy tensing again, building to a second orgasm in fucking record time.

The appetite we have for each other is impossible to feed. It's all-consuming and bordering on a sickness. When she's not near me, I don't feel complete.

"Give it to me, Alicia. I want to feel that perfect little cunt come for the second time," I order.

Alicia moans. "Yes, daddy," she rasps out as I choke her dainty little throat and fuck her at the same time.

Her orgasm comes suddenly as her entire body quivers and a gush of liquid floods my cock for the second time tonight.

Feeling her come for me again is all it takes to push me off the cliff's edge. I growl as a powerful, all-consuming climax slams into me.

I drain all my cum deep inside of her tight pussy. "That's it, baby, take daddy's seed like a good girl," I rasp, letting go of her throat and grabbing her hips, continuing to thrust long after I've climaxed.

I could keep going, keep fucking her all damn night without a moment to rest.

Alicia moans again, suggesting she feels exactly the same.

I can't stop. I won't stop. Instead, I want to drown myself in this feeling and never leave this room again.

---

THE LAST FEW days have been a whirlwind with Alicia.

Ever since the truth about my obsession with her

came out, she's more insatiable than ever. I can't deny that I worried that I'd lose her when I revealed the truth about my stalker-like tendencies before we hooked up. Alicia was reluctant at first, but it's clear she's as hooked on me as I am on her.

The office block towers above me as I get out of the Uber car. Malachy will be glad that I've finally cracked the mystery.

The Italians haven't used our docks since the feud began, leaving us scratching our heads over how they are still bringing in their product to the city. Malachy tasked me with finding out, and I've got the answer for him today.

Ever since I started sleeping with his sister, it's been harder to look him in the eye. Keeping something so huge from my best friend doesn't sit well with me. I know there has to come a time where we come clean, but I haven't dared bring it up with Alicia. She fears he will kill me if he finds out.

I run a hand through my hair and step forward, entering McCarthy headquarters, the investment company Malachy bought and renamed a few years ago as a front for his operations. Before that, the police were hot on our tail, trying to bring us down. Malachy had to buy out a few cops to ensure our troubles with the Boston PD went away.

"Morning, Mr. Fitzpatrick," Sue, the secretary, calls as I walk through the door.

I nod at her. "Morning."

She smiles as I head for the elevator. I often feel uncomfortable entering the McCarthy enterprises because it's so normal and legal. I get some odd looks when I come by because of the tattoos visible up the side of my neck over my suit. Everyone in here is on the straight and narrow, unaware of who exactly they're working for.

Malachy's office is on the top floor. The elevator opens, and I step onto the floor. Instantly I notice his door is ajar, and he's sitting at his desk, so I knock to get his attention. "Sir, can I come in?"

He nods.

I enter and sit opposite him. "We've worked out how the Italians are bringing in their product."

Malachy's eyes light up. "Perfect. I hope we can intercept."

On that front, I'm not sure my news is so good since the Russians run Salem. "They're bringing in product to the docks at Salem."

"Are you serious?" Mal shakes his head. "We can't block them without pissing off the Russians." He runs a hand across the back of his neck. "How do they get the drugs into the city?" I ask.

I sigh heavily, knowing that the mystery of where they are bringing their drugs in is just the tip of the iceberg. "Haulage trucks, but we can't seem to find a pattern in their routes. Every route they take is different." I scrub my jaw. "The Italians aren't stupid. They know they have to be careful at the moment."

Malachy slams his fist into the table before standing and pacing. "How are we going to strike back if they keep one step ahead of us all the time?"

I don't have the answer which will piss him off. "I don't know, sir. It seems like everything we think of, they've already taken precautions to stop."

Malachy inhales a deep breath. "Niall, I need you to help me out here, lad. I'm coming up blank."

"Maybe we don't hit his supply." I've been thinking about different ways to hit them for a while now, but they're risky. "The supply is only the start of the chain. Why don't we fuck up his laundering? That way, he can't clean any of his cash."

Malachy smiles. "You bloody genius." he laughs. "I've been so set on cutting off the supply. I haven't even thought about the chain." He pats me on the shoulder. It's rare he's so complimentary of my ideas, so he must really like this one. "That's why you are my second. Now, get that plan in motion with the guys and report back to me once done."

I nod, thankful that he likes my idea. "Aye, sir, on it." I can't deny that spending time around Malachy lately has been difficult. Every time I look him in the eye, I'm reminded of the fact I'm screwing his sister behind his back.

I stand and walk out of the room without a glance backward, knowing that despite my reservations over my relationship with his sister, a part of me won't let me stop. Alicia is everything to me. It would take

Malachy stabbing a knife through my heart to stop me from seeing her.

Perhaps that's exactly where this train wreck of an affair is heading, but all of the risks are worth the reward, no matter the outcome.

13

## ALICIA

*I* walk down the street, taking the long way to town, as I haven't ventured down by the river since Niall saved me from that rapist.

Jane is meeting me for lunch, and I seriously need to tell her everything. She's my best friend and the only person I can talk to about this.

It's crazy how many things have changed since I saw her three weeks ago at our mutual friend's party.

Niall has become my world in such a brief space of time, but Jane doesn't know the truth about my brother.

I'm pretty sure she's just going to tell me to rip the Band-Aid off and tell Malachy. It would be easy enough if he wasn't a murderous criminal with anger issues.

The Three Amigos is our favorite lunchtime spot.

As it comes into view, I can see Jane sitting at our usual table waiting for me.

I glance behind me, making sure no one is following me. Ever since Niall admitted to stalking me, I've been on edge. It's clear that I've been unaware of my surroundings for too long considering I haven't ever noticed him following me around.

The restaurant isn't too busy as I join Jane at our table.

"Hey, sorry, the walk took longer than I expected," I say, sitting down opposite her.

She smiles. "Don't worry about it. I ordered us margaritas," she says, gesturing at the two glasses. "I also put our usual order in already."

I nod. "Thanks."

Her brow furrows. "What's up with you?"

I shake my head. "So damn much, Jane. I do not know where to start."

She sits up straighter and her eyes widen. "Oh, I'm in need of some juicy gossip. Spill."

I swallow hard, wondering if it's a bad idea to tell Jane. It hasn't felt as real since no one else knows. Niall and I are in our own little bubble, safe from the judgement of the rest of the world.

"I slept with Niall," I say.

"Niall as in your brother's best friend?" she asks.

I nod, feeling heat pulsing through my cheeks. "Not just once either. I'm sleeping with him."

"Shit, Malachy won't be happy, right?" she asks.

She knows that my brother has orchestrated the downfall of many of my relationships. "I honestly don't know." I cast my mind back to the day he called me in to sign his will.

*I'm sorry that I've chased away men from your life in the past. I won't do it next time.*

"He said he was sorry for the way he treated the men in my life in the past." I shrug, sighing. "I just don't know what to do, Jane."

Jane grabs my hand and squeezes. "Is Niall the one?"

I contemplate her question, knowing I've always been skeptical about the belief that there is one right person for everyone. However, as I think about Niall and the way we are together, it makes the notion believable. It's as if we were made for each other. "Yes, I think I love him, Jane."

Jane squeals, beaming from ear to ear. "At last, it's about time you found a man to settle down with." Her expression turns sorrowful. "I hope it works out better for you."

I squeeze her hand. "You can't give up on being happy again."

She reclaims her hand and pushes a stray hair behind her ear. "I know. It's been six years since Darren died." She shakes her head. "It's just hard to think about finding anyone as amazing as him again."

My heart aches for her. Her husband was a lovely

guy, and I was bridesmaid at their wedding twenty years ago. They met in high school, but he died of cancer six years ago, leaving her a single mom to two young kids. "I can't imagine what it is like for you."

Jane nods. "It gets easier with time, but the thought of ever really finding someone to make me happy again feels impossible."

I consider that for a moment, believing that if Niall were to die I'm not sure how I'd be happy again. It feels like now we've found each other, I couldn't live without him. "I understand. Maybe if the right person comes along someday." I glance at my cell phone which buzzes, noticing the date.

It's the twenty-fourth, which means I'm six days late. "Hmm, that's weird," I murmur to myself.

"What's weird?"

I shake my head. "It's probably nothing. I'm six days late, but maybe I'm just starting menopause?"

Jane's brow furrows. "A bit early, have you and Niall been safe?"

I swallow hard, searching my friends eyes. Surely she can't think I'm pregnant. "I'm past all that."

"I don't think so, Alicia. You know Helen, she's three years older than you and got pregnant naturally."

The waiter appears with her food, setting my quesadillas down in front of me. Suddenly, I feel too sick to eat.

"Do you really think I could be pregnant?" I ask once he's left.

Jane shrugs. "Only one way to find out for sure. I assume from your reaction you guys haven't been careful?"

Our passion is too damn hot. Neither of us ever stopped to consider those repercussions. Every time that man touches me I lose my mind. "No, we haven't been."

"Eat your food and stop worrying. We will get a test afterwards," Jane says.

"I feel too queasy."

Jane laughs. "Since when does anything put you off quesadillas here?"

"Since I think I might be pregnant with my brother's best friend's baby."

"Yeah, that might be a bit of a nightmare, but forget about it. We can work this out after we eat." She shoves a nacho into her mouth, crunching on it.

I pick at my quesadilla, finding it hard to focus on anything but the idea of being pregnant.

*What the hell will I do if I am?*

At thirty-eight years old, I truly believed that was behind me. Over the years I'd given thought to being a mother, but knew it was probably a bad idea.

*How can I be a good mother when I barely knew my own?*

Malachy raised me on the streets, and this world we live in isn't right for a child, I know that firsthand. All I can do is hope that it's not a problem I need to face.

I glance out of the window of the restaurant and my heart skips a beat when I see those familiar, ice-blue eyes staring right at me. Niall sits in the cafe opposite in the window, watching me.

"Fuck," I say.

Jane shakes her head. "What is it? You're not going to be sick, are you?'

"No, one thing I left out about Niall. He's kind of a head case."

Her brow furrows. "A head case, how?"

I fill her in on the fact he's being stalking me before pointing out the fact he's spying on the both of us right now.

"Shit, that's pretty messed up, Alicia." It's not often that Jane swears. "Are you sure this relationship isn't a little bit toxic?"

I'm not sure of anything anymore. The way we want each other so desperately probably is bordering on toxic, but then can something be toxic if it makes you feel better than you've ever felt?

"Who knows? All I know is I'm in love with him and he loves me." I shrug. "It just freaks me out a little, especially as I need to work out if I'm pregnant without him sniffing around."

"I have an idea." Jane's eyes light up. "We part ways and you go home. I'll grab a test and meet you at the house in forty minutes. What about that?"

I'm not sure what I'd do without Jane. We've been through a lot together, supported each other through our adult lives. "You are a damn lifesaver."

She smiles. "It's nothing. Finish up your food, we'll settle the bill and then carry out the plan." She glances over at the restaurant again, looking at Niall. "I still can't believe the guy you are fucking is following you though. Don't you find it creepy?"

I don't know anymore. All I can think about is the fact I could be pregnant with his baby. "I guess," I say, digging in to the rest of my food.

Our relationship is complicated enough without adding a possible accidental pregnancy into the mix. Niall isn't the kind of man who wants kids. I know that because of a conversation we had when we were younger, the three of us.

He's a lone wolf and before we got together, I never saw him with the same girl more than once. I know his past haunts him. The question is: will it also haunt our future?

---

THE BELL RINGS and I rush to the door, thankful to find Jane there holding a drugstore bag. "Right on time," she says, glancing behind her. "He's not here, is he?"

I open the door wider. "No, luckily. I rang him to make sure, and he's at the office."

"I hope you also called him out on stalking you."

I draw in a deep breath as I tried to. Niall shut me down with his intoxicatingly dominant charm. Every time he orders me around, I turn into an eager puppet for him. "Kind of. Follow me."

Jane rarely comes over to my place because I don't want to risk her finding out the dark secret that shrouds our family. The crime which Malachy sometimes brings back here. "Wow, this place is as amazing as I remember. Why do we never hang out here?"

"Because my brother can be a real asshole," I say.

She laughs. "The same brother you were trying to set me up with, right?"

In hindsight, it was a terrible idea. I just want Malachy to have a proper, meaningful relationship for once in his life. "Yeah, sorry." I shake my head. "That wasn't one of my brightest ideas. Luckily, you both refused."

Jane follows me to my room, and I lock the door behind us. "I think I'm going to pass out I'm so nervous."

My friend grabs my hand and steadies me. "Don't worry. I've got you." She leads me to the edge of my bed, and I sit. "Just take your time. I've got all afternoon."

"Thank God you are here. I don't know how I'd do this without you." I glance at the drugstore bag, feeling the anxiety twist at my gut. "I best just get this over and done with."

"If that's what you want." Her brow furrows. "Do you want me to come in—"

I shake my head. "No, I'm fine. Give me a minute." I grab the bag and head into the bathroom, shutting the door. My head is spinning as I rest my back against it, pulling the test out.

This is totally crazy. I do the test and put the cap back on, feeling more fearful than I've felt in all my life. The mere idea of having to break this news to Niall makes me sick. It will burst the blissful bubble we've been in the past couple of weeks.

A bubble I never want out of.

"How you getting on in there?" Jane calls.

I open the door, leaving the test on the counter. "It's done. I'm just too scared to look."

Jane grabs me and pulls me into a hug. "Don't worry, everything is going to be okay. Trust me."

Tears prickle my eyes and I allow them to fall, wrapping my arms around Jane. She's always been a rock for me, motherly. Even though we're basically the same age minus a year.

"Do you want me to look at it for you?" she asks.

I nod in response, wiping away my tears. "Please be negative," I murmur under my breath.

Jane picks up the test and from the look on her face, she doesn't need to tell me.

"Positive?" I ask.

Jane nods. "Yes."

A tense silence floods the air. It feels like my world

is spinning as I try to process the news. I'm pregnant with my brother's best friend's baby. I thought our relationship couldn't be any more complicated, but I was terribly wrong.

14

## NIALL

*A*licia is lying on the sofa in the library, a book in her hand and her hair splayed over the cream fabric delicately. She is as flawless as an angel.

"Hey," I say, catching her attention.

I notice the tension coil through her at the sound of my voice. The usual, serene smile she gives me is nowhere to be seen.

Alicia sits up. "Hey." She crosses her arms over her chest.

I can only imagine this has something to do with her realizing I was spying on her with her friend. It was a stupid decision. Something I knew I shouldn't do, but old habits die hard.

I shut the door and approach her. "What's up?" I ask.

She shakes her. "Nothing."

"Don't lie to me, little lass. I know something is up

with you." I sigh heavily as I sit next to her, noticing that she inches away from me. "Is it because I followed you to the restaurant?"

Alicia's lips purse together tightly. "Possibly. I thought that was over now that we're fucking."

I grab her hand and squeeze it. "Is it so bad that I want to protect you at all times?"

She yanks her hand away. "I don't need protecting, Niall."

Anger ignites inside of me at her cold refusal of my advances. "It didn't seem that way when I had to kill a man who almost raped you."

The mention of my rescue of her down by the river hits a nerve as she stands and walks away from me. "You are a psycho."

I can't understand why she's being like this. When she found out that I followed her for years, it didn't bother her. The moment she sees me sitting in the cafe opposite the restaurant, she loses her shit.

It doesn't add up.

"Are you sure that is what's wrong?" I ask, standing and following her.

She turns around to face me. "Of course. What else would it be?"

"It doesn't make sense. When you found out how much I knew about you, you were more insatiable than ever. Why the sudden change of heart?"

She stares at me for a few beats. "Jane thinks we're toxic, and I agree."

A deep growl rises through my gut, rumbling through my chest. I charge at her, grabbing her hips hard and pushing her against the bookcase. "I'll kill her," I say, knowing in my gut that I mean it. I'll kill anyone that tries to split us up.

"Niall, it's not her fault. I—"

"Bullshit. You left me this morning walking on cloud nine. Now you can barely look me in the eye." I grab her chin and force her eyes to meet mine. "Jane has gotten in your head."

My possessive inclination with Alicia makes it impossible to act like a sane human being.

Alicia holds her head high. "You are acting like a maniac. Do you realize that?"

I nod in response, moving my hand to her throat and gripping it. "I do, because that's what you do to me, Alicia." I press my lips to her ear and whisper, "You make me fucking crazy like no one else can."

Her slender throat bobs beneath my hand. "Niall," she breathes my name, and it's a sound of pure desperation.

"What do you want, little lass?" I ask, leaning back to search her stunning emerald eyes.

There's a war raging in their depths, but she finally speaks, "You."

The moment those words leave her lips, I snap.

I lift her against the bookcase, forcing her to grab hold of me. All common sense is gone, and I can't even remember if I locked the door.

It doesn't matter. All that matters is being inside the beauty in front of me.

I unzip my pants and nudge her thong out of the way, too desperate to remove it right now.

Alicia groans the moment I slide inside of her soaking wet pussy.

I lift her up and down my cock, moving her delicate frame as she takes everything I give her.

Our bodies come together in a violent clash of skin as we forget about everything else but each other. Both of us hold each other's gaze, and that intimate connection that runs so deep sets my soul on fire.

If there's one thing I'm certain about, I'd rather die than let this woman go. She is my world. My everything. If she ever tried to break this off, I don't know what I'd do.

---

I KNOW how dangerous this is.

Milo Mazzeo isn't someone you want to get caught fucking with. He is as sadistic as my best friend and that's saying something.

Oisin and Patrick step to either side of me, and Conor lingers a short way behind, as we wait for the signal from Brian and Rory that it's time to move inside. One of Mazzeo's biggest money laundering sites is his central Boston club, Le Mura. Milo shut it down for refurbishments this week, meaning it's our best time to strike. The construction company has today off according to one of my contacts, meaning it's our only window of opportunity.

Milo would expect us to attack him at night, so we're doing it in the day. It's a risk we all agreed on. As I stand in the alleyway behind the club waiting for the signal, I can't help but doubt myself. Malachy asked me to take charge of this, so I didn't run it by him. If it all goes wrong, it's on me.

A crackle on the radio enters my ear. "It's all clear from our angle," Rory says.

I bring my receiver to my mouth. "Grand, we all go in together. How about your side, Craig and Oscar?"

I tap my foot on the pavement, waiting for the reply.

"Aye, all clear from our side too," Craig replies.

I draw in a deep, steadying breath before giving the order into the receiver. "Okay, clear to move. Stick to the plan. We need to be in and out fast." Patrick pulls out his kit to pick the lock and makes quick work of unlocking the club. The moment it unlocks, the alarm beeps counting down the thirty seconds to disarm it. Alarms are Oisin's forte as he steps forward and pulls the cover off the keypad, working hastily to disarm the unit without setting the alarm off.

I pat him on the back as it stops beeping. "Good work, lad."

Oisin smirks. "Works every time." Oisin is

Malachy's cousin. I can't deny I had mixed feelings when he brought his father's brother's family into the business. For a start, they knew he and Alicia were on the streets as kids and did nothing. They didn't have the money to look after them, apparently, but I think it's bullshit. If your family is on the street, you do whatever it takes to protect them.

Malachy believes family is important and brought his uncle into the business, along with his cousins. All except for Darragh, who is in jail and a fucking psychopath.

"Now, you all know your roles. Get it done fast."

I notice Brian and Rory already getting to work on the mezzanine of the club, setting up explosives. We have to ensure the place is out of action for a long time, which means blowing it apart. It's a large building, so we need to cover a few key areas to ensure we're successful.

"Aye, see you in five," Conor says, taking off with Patrick to his allocated section of the club. Conor is always cocky. The likelihood that he can set up the explosives that fast is slim.

Oisin meets my gaze. "Ready?"

I nod, but I can't help the unease that sweeps over the back of my neck as I follow him down the corridor toward the back office. It would be a waste to blow any cash the Italians might have stashed in the club, so we are going to do a sweep before setting up the explosives in the office. If we can take from them and blow their laundering operation apart, then all the better.

Oisin stops in front of the door and tries it. It's locked. "Bust it in?" he asks.

I nod and step back as he pulls a gun out of his pocket and shoots into the barrel of the lock. It breaks apart and Oisin kicks open the door. My heart sinks the moment I see what is waiting for us.

Mazzeo's men are gathered in the office with their guns drawn.

"Shit," Oisin says, followed by a round going off.

I watch in shock as the bullet hits him right between the eyes and blood splatters the air. He drops to the floor, lifeless. Time slows as the sound of another shot sends adrenaline pulsing through my veins. I fling myself to the floor, away from the door, but the bullet clips my leg.

I growl before pushing myself onto my feet and sprinting as fast as I can toward the back entrance of the club. Gun shots in the distance suggest there's more of them in the club. Conor is waiting by the side door, holding his hand to his neck. Our eyes meet and I know instantly he's been shot. "I ain't going to make it, lad, get the fuck out of here," he says.

I shake my head and grab his shoulders. "You need to fight. Where's Patrick?"

His eyes mist with sadness, and he shakes his head. "The bastards shot him right through the heart. He's gone."

Rory and Brian rush toward us, both limping with blood splattering their shirts. "Fuck, is anyone not injured?" I shake my head. "You two help Conor out to the van and get the engine running. If I'm not there in five minutes, you leave."

"No way," Rory says.

I glare at him, feeling rage infect my blood. "It's an order," I say, infusing as much threat as I can. If I were Malachy, they wouldn't dare question me.

He pales and nods. "Fine, but you better be quick."

Brian gets on the left-hand side of Conor and Rory on the right as they help him out of the club. It feels insane walking further into danger, but I can't leave two of my men inside. It's not what our clan is about.

A commotion coming from the left-hand side of the dance floor draws my attention. Gun shots follow the shouting.

*Fuck.*

Malachy is going to kill me if I make it out of here alive. Normally I'm the level-headed one for making plans, but on this occasion I royally screwed up. This couldn't have gone down any worse.

I rush toward the gun shots and collide with Craig, practically dragging a badly injured Oscar. "Shit, you're both shot." I grab the other side of Oscar. "Let's get the hell out of here fast."

A gun cocks behind us, making both of us freeze. "Not so fast."

The hair on the back of my neck stands on end at the sound of Milo's unmistakable voice. "Get him out of here." I look Craig in the eye, and he looks uncertain. "Now," I order.

I turn to face the clan's enemy, looking him in the eye. "What do you want?" I know the only way to get out of here alive is to negotiate. The trouble is I haven't got the authority to agree to a truce.

He tilts his head to the side. "Niall Fitzpatrick, right?"

I swallow hard, nodding. "Yeah."

"I'm not sure you can offer me anything." A cruel smirk twists onto his lips. "Killing you, however, would send a damn good message."

My heart pounds so hard it feels like it might tear through my chest at any moment. I stare down the barrel of the gun, knowing that this is without a doubt the most dangerous situation I've been in. Which is saying something considering I lived on the streets for six years.

As I stare death in the face, the one person who comes to my mind is Alicia. I can't die now, not when we've only just embraced what has always existed between us.

"I could negotiate terms of a truce with Malachy for you," I suggest, knowing that I'm clutching at straws. My only chance is to buy myself time. A few men come rushing down the corridor, joining their boss.

I take an instinctive step backward, feeling threatened. Milo shoots me without hesitation, hitting me in the stomach. The pain is excruciating as I drop to the floor, racking my brain for a way out of this. I turn and crawl behind the bar as fast as I can, but Milo shoots my other leg.

"Fuck," I growl, pulling myself behind the bar before he can shoot me again.

The minutes are ticking away, and if Rory listened to me, then they have probably already left. I clench my jaw, trying to work out how to get out of this club.

Then it hits me. I'm still clutching hold of the bag with the explosives in. It's a crazy idea, but I'm desperate. I pull the bomb out of the bag, knowing I can't rig it to explode. The only way to use it is to throw it at them and then shoot it, using this bar as cover.

Unless they believe it's rigged when I throw it, which might buy me enough time to make a run for it. Either way, it's all I've got. I fling the bomb at them.

"Cazzo," I hear someone shout. "Take cover."

I smirk as they clearly think it's rigged. Quickly, I jump to my feet and make a run for it, hoping they won't realize that it's a dud.

As I run toward the exit someone shouts, "He's getting away." A gunshot follows, and it hits me in the shoulder.

"Fuck," I growl, running for the exit despite the agony coursing through my body. The adrenaline makes it possible as I notice the van parked outside with the engine running.

Fucking idiots ignored me. An odd sensation of thankfulness and irritation claws at me. If they hadn't ignored me, I'd be a dead man. I grit my teeth together as the pain becomes unbearable, but I know I have to push through. The sprint to the van almost kills me as my head swims.

The back of the van is open, and Rory is there, holding a hand out to me. I grab hold of it, and he yanks me into the van. I slam into the floor of it, grunting at the excruciating pain. Craig slams the doors shut as Derrick puts his foot down, jolting us against the wall of the van. I groan as we escape the bloodbath, holding a hand to one of my wounds to stem the blood flow.

"Shit, how many times were you hit?" Rory asks.

I shake my head, feeling my head spin. Three, four, five times, I'm not even sure anymore. I don't have the strength to reply as I shut my eyes, focusing on drawing enough oxygen into my lungs, despite the pain coursing through my flesh. The only way I make it through this is if I conserve energy until Alastair can patch me up.

As I remain on the floor of the van with my eyes shut and bleeding out, Alicia's angelic face springs into my mind. I need to make it through this so that I can see her again.

Delirium hits me fast as I feel her presence and reach out toward her. "Alicia," I murmur her name before succumbing to the pull of unconsciousness as everything turns black.

## 15

## ALICIA

My world is spinning as I stare at the man I've finally fallen for lying lifeless in a hospital bed. The man whose baby is growing inside of me. It's been two days since I found out, but I haven't had the guts to tell Niall.

I clutch onto his hand, wishing he would wake up.

The fear I felt when I heard the Italians had shot him was insurmountable. I want to know why the fuck Malachy sent him into such a dangerous situation with the Italians. According to Alistair, the surgeon, they shot him four times. He said he was lucky to have lived.

Tears flood down my cheeks as I clutch his hand in mine.

"Please make it through, Niall. I can't live without you," I murmur quietly.

Alistair said he was through the worst of it, but that he needs to be observed. I intend to spend the entire night by his side. I may as well put the nursing degree I got to good use.

"Sis, what are you doing down here?"

I practically jump out of my seat, dropping Niall's hand in shock. Malachy's brow pulls together as he stares at me questioningly.

"I heard what happened and wanted to see if I could help at all." I glance back at Niall. "I can't believe Niall got caught up in this. Why did you send your best man to do such a dangerous job?"

*Why did he send the love of my life into a war zone?*

The father of the baby growing inside of me. Malachy would kill both of us if he knew the truth. When I glance back at Malachy, I can see the frustration on his face. "I left him in charge of cutting the fucking Italians off by shutting down their laundering operations across the city." Malachy shakes his head, attention fixed on Niall. "He came up with the idea and organized it. I didn't tell him to be on the front line, for fuck's sake."

The entire situation is overwhelming, and coupled with Malachy's angry tone of voice, the floodgates open. Tears roll down my cheeks relentlessly. I hate crying in front of my brother. I know he sees me as this vulnerable little girl, but I can't hold it in any longer.

"What is it to you anyway?" Malachy asks, his

head tilted slightly. "You knew Niall when we were kids, but I didn't think you were close anymore."

*Is he insane?*

Niall practically lives at this house. "Of course we are. Niall's in this house as much as you are, if not more." My brother is so often wrapped up in his own world he misses everything that goes on around him. It's a blessing, considering Niall and I have been sneaking around behind his back.

Malachy strolls to Niall's bed and glances down at him. "Whoever did this, I'll fucking kill them, Niall."

I watch as Malachy places a hand on his shoulder.

"Someone betrayed us to the Italians, and they will pay."

It's a worrying sentiment. The last thing I need is for Malachy to come in here next, shot half to death. I move to stand on the opposite side of the bed. "Is violence always your answer, Brother?"

Malachy's bright green eyes meet mine and they are full of dangerous rage. "That's a stupid question, Alicia."

I know that it's always been Malachy's answer. He doesn't know how to win battles without physical violence. I slump into the chair next to Niall's bed. "Why was Niall in charge, anyway?" I glance back up at my brother. "Where were you?"

"I was taking a day off," Malachy replies. There's guilt written all over his face.

"With the virgin that you bought at the auction?" I ask.

Malachy's jaw clenches. "Yeah, what of it?"

"There's something different about this one, isn't there?" I shake my head. "I mean, when I saw her contentedly walking the grounds without a scratch or bruise on her, I knew there had to be."

Malachy glares at me. "I don't know what you're talking about."

He always has been so fucking secretive. I laugh, though, as it's clear she's under his skin. "I hope she will finally be the end of your sick and twisted obsessions with those auctions. She seems like a nice girl."

My comment earns me a growl. "Yes, a girl you told my life fucking story to."

I hold my hands up. "We merely had a conversation. Girl to girl."

Malachy's knuckles are turning white as he balls them into fists. "Well, don't in the future. I don't want you talking to Scarlett, do you understand?"

I raise a brow. "Wow, you have it bad for her, Mal." I know he hates me calling him that.

"Whatever," he grunts, turning away and looking at the other casualties in the infirmary.

All my attention moves back to Niall, who looks so broken. Malachy questions the other men and doctors, but I hardly hear what they're saying. I could have lost Niall today. It's hard to believe that I've been so blind all these years to the man who has been there for me.

I hear Malachy call out to Alistair. "Alistair, do you need help tonight?"

Alistair meets his gaze and nods. "Yes, I can't deal with the five by myself. If you can send a couple of guys to give me a hand, that would be grand."

My brother orders Seamus to sort it out, but I have every intention of offering to help. It's the least I can do, especially since I will be here all night anyway. This way it is less suspicious if I'm supposed to be down here. "I'll help here tonight. It's the least I can do," I say once Seamus is gone, glancing at my brother.

Alistair smiles. "That would be great, Alicia, since you're a trained nurse."

"Yes, it makes sense for me to help instead of some knuckleheads that don't know what they're doing."

Malachy stares at me with narrowed eyes. If he's suspicious, he doesn't voice it. "Fine, but don't be overworking yourself, Sis." He turns to leave. "I'll see you all tomorrow."

I watch as my brother walks away, acting as if nothing has happened. He doesn't know how to deal with something like this because he's scared. Niall is like a brother to him. I know losing Niall would hurt him almost as badly as it would hurt me.

Alistair clears his throat. "Can you check the

patient's vitals and administer their IV fluids while I head upstairs and grab something to eat? I've been at it none stop for twelve hours, as Aiden called me after my shift at the hospital."

I nod. "Of course, maybe try to have an hour or two of sleep. I can call you if there's anything urgent."

Alistair smiles at me. "Thanks. What would I do without you?"

I shrug. "Be exhausted and hungry, I guess."

He laughs and walks away. "My phone is on. Call me if you need me."

I turn around and glance at the room full of sleeping, injured men. Apparently one man, Conor, died on the way back here. There was nothing they could do for him, as he'd lost too much blood. Oisin, our cousin, died in the club and there was no way to get him out without risking everyone else's lives. Our uncle will be unbelievably angry now that his only living son is a psychopath locked up in prison. Tears flood my eyes as I watch Niall knowing that it could have been him that died on the way here or in the club instead of Oisin.

I walk to his side and sit in the chair, grabbing his hand. "Please be okay, Niall," I murmur, bringing his hand to my lips and kissing it. I know that there is no way I can do this without him. He's my rock. I do not know how to be a mother. The thought of facing that by myself makes me sick. "You mean everything to me." All I know is there's no way I would have an abortion, even though Jane suggested it.

Niall groans softly in his sleep, igniting hope inside of me. "Alicia," he murmurs my name.

Tears well in my eyes as I stand and cup his face in my hands. "I'm here, Niall."

His eyes flicker open, and he groans again. "I feel like I've died."

"You almost did." I feel the tears rolling down my cheeks. "I can't believe you were so reckless."

He breathes deeply. "Someone betrayed us. Milo knew to expect us there." He tries to sit up, but I stop him.

"No, Niall. You need to rest. Alastair had you in surgery less than an hour ago."

Niall rests back and shuts his eyes. "The last thing I saw before I passed out was your face. I was so scared I'd never see you again," he says.

His words are like an arrow to my heart as tears spill down my cheeks faster. At first, I wondered if this was just about sex for him, but it's clear we both feel something deeper. This isn't just a couple of people fucking, we care for each other deeply.

"Niall, I thought you were going to die." I grab hold of his hand and kiss the back of it. "I've never been so scared in my life either."

Niall's eyes flicker open and he pats the side of the hospital bed, signaling for me to get on it with him.

I glance around, making sure the other men are

still unconscious. Once I'm confident they are, I get onto the bed next to him. My head rests on his good shoulder, and I listen to the soothing beat of his heart. "Never risk your life like that again," I murmur, feeling the fear I felt when I found out return with overwhelming strength. "I can't lose you."

Niall laces his fingers in my hair and angles my face to look at him. "I promise, little lass. I'll be more careful."

I search his eyes, knowing without a doubt he means it with every fiber of his being. "Niall," I whisper his name, drawing him closer.

Our lips touch in a tentative, heartfelt kiss that makes me feel like we're the only two people on this planet. A bang breaks us both apart.

I glance over to see Rory is awake and staring right at us. His glass of water is knocked on the floor by his bed. I jump off of Niall's bed and rush over to collect it.

"Shit, I thought I heard you say Alicia's name in the back of the van," Rory says, making me tense. "I had hoped it was a different Alicia."

I glance over at Niall, whose eyes turn cold as he glares at the man in the opposite bed. "You didn't hear or see anything, do you understand?" The threat in his voice is clear.

Rory holds his hands up, wincing. "Of course, lad. I'm no snitch but be careful." He shakes his head. "You know what would happen if Malachy finds out."

The warning drags me right out of the fantasy and back into reality. Malachy will kill Niall for touching me. Not because he doesn't trust his best friend, but because it's a direct betrayal of his trust on both our parts. Malachy's biggest hate is people lying to him.

Now, I'm not only lying to my brother, but I'm keeping the truth from Niall as well. Fear over his reaction makes it almost impossible to tell him I'm carrying his baby.

I fear that the web of lies we're both spinning will catch up to both of us sooner rather than later.

16

# NIALL

Silence fills the room as the rest of the men in the ward sleep. I can't keep my eyes off of Rory as he sleeps in the bed opposite.

Alicia has gone for a break to grab something to eat. The threat of him knowing our lie only heightens my concern. Rory and I don't know each other that well, so I can't be sure that I can trust him.

He knows the truth that could end everything for Alicia and me. I need to make sure he understands that if he outs me, I'll fucking kill him and his family with my bare hands.

I wince as I get out of my hospital bed, grabbing hold of the IV pole for support. It helps make it easier to steady myself as I creep toward his bed. Once I get there, I sit down in the chair next to him.

At first, he doesn't wake up and continues to snore

loudly. I stare at him for a few moments, contemplating whether threatening this man to keep him quiet is the best plan. It's all I know. He has the chance to tear our world apart.

I will not risk everything I care about over some lowlife clan member. I shake him roughly, waking him.

His eyes open wide. "What the—"

I place my hand over his mouth. "Keep your voice down."

Rory nods in response, looking fearful.

I remove my hand. "We need to have a chat, man to man."

His brow furrows. "If this is about you and Alicia, I told you that I'm no snitch."

I run a hand across the back of my neck. "How can I be sure, aye? We don't know each other very well." I tilt my head. "Why would you keep this secret from the boss?"

Rory sits up in bed straighter. "I'll keep it because I know what it's like to fall in love with the wrong person, lad."

I know he has a wife and children, but I know little about his life story. "How so?"

Rory sighs heavily. "My wife was my brother's girl in high school. They were together for four years."

That is even worse than our situation, although I doubt his brother was an unhinged criminal mastermind who always reacts with violence. "Shit, that must have been rough."

"Yes, it was. My brother still won't talk to me to this day." He shrugs. "Unfortunately, what I found with Kelly was too precious to let go." There's sadness in his eyes as he speaks. "I still love my brother though. Even if this isn't something he can come to terms with."

I don't know what would happen if Malachy can't accept our relationship. Maybe he would kick me out of the clan and disown Alicia if she came with me. The thought instills fear in me as the clan is all I've known since the streets. "I don't know how Malachy will react." I run a hand through my hair. "He's not got a good track record with Alicia's lovers."

"I don't envy you." Rory gives me a sympathetic look. "Luckily, my brother wasn't the type to murder either of us over it." His brow pulls together. "But you and Malachy have known each other for years, right?"

"Right. Not sure that will make it any better." I sigh and meet his gaze. "Just know that if you even think about spilling your guts, I know where you and your family live."

Rory's eyes flash with anger, but he reins it in. "Look, lad, there's no need to threaten me. I have no interest in fucking this up for you."

I wince as I sit up straighter, wondering if it was a

mistake getting out of bed in the first place. "Good. Alicia means everything to me. I'd die for her."

Rory chuckles. "Believe me, I know the feeling."

I hold my hand out for him to shake. "It was good talking to you."

He shakes my hand firmly. "You too. Word of advice, come clean sooner rather than later." There's clear regret in his expression. "My brother won't speak to me because of the way we handled it. He had to learn from someone else, rather than us having the guts to tell him to his face. That's what hurt him the most."

I nod and stand, using the IV pole for support. "Thanks." Rory is right. I know that Malachy will be more upset that this has been going on behind his back. I get back into bed and shut my eyes, instantly seeing Alicia's angelic face.

There is one thing I know for sure. Alicia and I are in it for the long hall. This isn't just a fling to me, it means everything.

It means that telling Malachy sooner rather than later is our best plan of action. The only question is, how are we going to ensure he doesn't kill me in the process?

We may be like brothers, but this is the first time I've ever done something to break his trust this badly.

A part of me hopes that he's happy for us, but I know Malachy. He's got a shorter fuse than anyone. Alicia has been his responsibility since he was a little kid, and he takes that responsibility a little too seriously. I'm not sure he'll be too happy about passing the reins over to me.

There's only one way to find out.

---

A week has passed since the Italians shot me. My wounds are healing well. Alastair is one of the best surgeons in the city, so there were no complications getting the bullets out of me.

Alicia visits every day, but it's getting increasingly difficult not to fuck her down here. Especially since I'm the only one left on the ward now. All the other guys had superficial flesh wounds, whereas mine were more serious.

"How are you feeling today, Niall?" Alastair asks, holding his clipboard in his hand.

"As good as new, lad. When can I get out of here?"

Alastair raises a brow, shaking his head. "Your vitals are good, but the injuries you sustained traditionally would be monitored for at least a few more days."

I sigh heavily. "Come on Alastair, I would rather be in my room upstairs." I rub a hand across the back of my neck. "Alicia can always monitor me and check my vitals."

Alastair sighs. "Yes, I bet you would love that."

I tense at the comment. "What's that supposed to mean?"

He raises a brow. "Do you think I'm fucking stupid, Niall? I've seen the way she is with you."

*Fuck.*

Somehow our secret is unraveling day by day. It's only a matter of time until Malachy learns the truth. "What are you saying, lad?" I ask, clenching my fist by my side. If I were well, I'd intimidate his ass to keep him quiet.

Alastair shakes his head and holds up his hands in surrender. "Look Niall, it's none of my business. You have nothing to worry about from me, but you need to be careful." He glances toward the door to ensure no one is approaching. "Malachy isn't very forgiving. You of all people know that."

I nod, confident that Alastair isn't the kind of guy to snitch. "Thank you. I know. We will figure it out."

Alastair doesn't look convinced, but he smiles. "Look, I'll take one last test and if I'm satisfied with the results, I'll discharge you to your room this afternoon."

"Great, lad. I appreciate it." I am going out of my mind, stuck down here. All I want is to sleep by her side again, holding her close to me.

I grab my cell phone off the nightstand.

*Alastair has agreed to release me today if my test results are good. I want a twenty-four-hour nurse, please.*

I fire the text to Alicia, waiting for her reply.

*Niall, I can't. My essay is due tomorrow.*

The blunt refusal cuts me deep.

*You told me it was finished two days ago. Alastair said I need to be monitored.*

The bubbles ignite, proving she's typing back. Then they disappear.

I grit my teeth together, frustrated that she's being like this. She'll regret refusing me once I get my hands on her later. Soon enough she'll forget all about her stupid essay.

Alastair takes a vial of my blood from a vein before heading off to test it, leaving me alone with my thoughts.

I put down my cell phone, giving up on receiving a reply.

Alicia has been off ever since she caught me spying on her and her friend. Perhaps she really believes that what we have is toxic. After all, no normal relationship starts with stalking.

Alicia needs to understand that my obsession with her was always born from a deep need to care for her. A need that persists to this day.

When we first met, I saved her from a terrible fate. Now, I want the chance to protect her as my own. Alicia belongs to me, and the sooner she accepts that, the better.

Alastair returns a few minutes later, smiling. "Your vitals are excellent." He walks over to me and places the clipboard at the bottom of the bed. "I'll just redress your wounds, and then you will be ready. Take your shirt off."

I wince as I pull my shirt over my head, remaining upright.

Alastair undoes the bandages to check the wounds. He cleans them with saline solution, which hurts like a bitch. Once they are clean, he wraps them with fresh bandages. "You can put your shirt back on."

I pull my shirt over my head.

"Your wounds are healing well. I thought you'd be off your feet for at least a month, but another week in bed and you can probably move around more." Alastair's eyes narrow. "No working though."

I nod. "Grand news."

"Shall I call Alicia?" he asks.

I shake my head, knowing that she has no intention of being my round the clock nurse. "Nah, I texted her and she's out at the moment," I lie. "Can you call Seamus and ask him to move me?"

He stares at me thoughtfully for a moment. "Can you promise me Alicia will check in on you?"

I clench my jaw. "Yes, why wouldn't she?"

"You are a terrible liar, Niall. If she isn't going to be checking you, I'll get a nurse to do it." He sighs. "I'll organize one to come by in two hours."

I swing my legs over the edge of the bed, wincing. "Alicia will check on me. No need to arrange another nurse." She may have refused, but I won't take no for an answer.

I'm not one to lie around in bed when I feel fine, except for a bit of pain. I have a girl to find and punish. The prospect of the chase thrills me almost as much as the thought of what I'm going to do to her when I find her.

17

ALICIA

Sasha steps in my path on the way to the kitchen. "Hey, Alicia. Got a minute?" she asks.

My brow furrows, as she never wants to speak with me. "Sure, what's up?"

She digs her cell phone out of her pocket and steps forward. "I know everything." She shows me an image of Niall fucking me against the bookcase in the library from before he was shot.

My stomach feels like a lead weight. "What do you want?"

"It's simple, really. Break it off with Niall, or your brother receives these anonymously."

Rage slams into me as I stare at the blonde bimbo, wondering how she thinks she has the right to threaten me. "Do you realize who I am?"

She smirks at me. "Alicia McCarthy, spoiled sister

of a rich and successful man. You are nothing but a leech."

Her words only stoke the fire of anger blazing to life inside of me. The last thing that I am is spoiled. If this stuck-up bitch knew half of what Malachy and I had been through on the street… I contain my rage, keeping my fist clenched by my side. "Why do you want me to break it off with him?"

She folds her arms over her chest. "Because Niall is mine. I was actually getting somewhere until you stepped in the way."

I laugh at that. "Are you serious? The night you delivered our pizza I asked him why he didn't date you and he said he wasn't interested."

"You're lying. We were fucking two months before you two had your little pizza and movie date."

My stomach twists hearing her say that Niall slept with her. It's crazy the jealous rage that washes over me, but as it takes hold I know I have no control over it.

I charge for her, grabbing her stupid blonde hair and slamming my fist into her face. "No one touches him but me." I force her against the wall and punch her again, making her scream.

The commotion draws attention as staff come to her aid. "Alicia, stop," Malachy shouts, grabbing hold of my shoulders and dragging me away from her. "What the hell are you doing?"

Sasha stands up, face cut from where I hit her.

"Nothing, she was being a dick, so I punched her."

Malachy turns and looks at Sasha. "I will deal with you later. Go to first aid and they will patch you up."

Sasha gives me a smug smirk once his back is turned and waves her phone in warning. "Sure, speak later."

I have never hated someone as much as I hate her. Malachy leads me into the sitting room off the corridor. "Sit," he orders.

I do as he says, knowing that it's going to be difficult to explain this to him, especially since our altercation was the result of a secret relationship I'm having with his best friend. "Start speaking, Alicia. What has gotten into you?"

I shake my head. "She was being a dick, chatting shit about me, and I snapped." I meet his gaze. "You should know all about that."

His brow furrows. "Yes, I do, but it's not like you to pick fights with people." He approaches and sits next to me on the couch. "Tell me what is wrong."

"Who says there is anything wrong?"

Malachy tuts. "I can see it written all over your face. Did you forget that I know you better than anyone else on this planet, Sis?"

I did forget it, because I don't think that is the truth—not anymore. Niall knows me like no one ever has. He sees me in ways I can hardly comprehend, and I see him.

We're made for each other, even if there are many complicated obstacles in our way. Sasha became another one on a long list.

She could ruin everything if she squealed. I know he will be pissed if we come out and tell him the truth, but finding out from someone else would be the icing on the cake.

He needs to hear it from Niall and me, but right now isn't the time. I need to discuss it with Niall before I tell the truth.

"I'm really stressed about my final exam next week." I let my head rest in my hands as my shoulders slump. It's a half truth, since I've not been studying enough. Not since Niall and I hooked up.

Malachy doesn't look convinced, after all he's known me all my life. "Why are you stressed. You know you are the smartest in your class."

That may have been true before I started sleeping with Niall, but that's because I devoted every waking moment to studying hard, when students half my age were out partying. "I have been feeling really tired lately. It's hampered my studying."

Malachy pulls me against him, wrapping his arms around me. "Don't worry. I believe you can do it. You're the smartest person I know."

I smile and hug my brother back, despite the guilt I feel at keeping the truth from him.

Niall was released today from the hospital wing, which means I need to address the issue with him tonight. I know suggesting we tell Malachy makes our relationship more serious, and I'm not sure that's what Niall wants.

When I told Jane I think I love him, I meant it. The question is whether or not he loves me back.

Someone clears their throat at the door, startling us both.

"Niall, what the fuck are you doing out of bed?" Malachy asks.

My eyes widen as I glance at the man I've fallen so desperately for. This is the first time the three of us have been in the same room since our affair started. It makes me anxious.

He shrugs, leaning on the doorframe for support. "Alastair agreed to release me to my room. When I heard the commotion, I thought someone was dying."

To be honest, the way Sasha squealed was ridiculous.

Malachy shakes his head. "You shouldn't be out of bed, lad."

Niall's eyes meet mine. "Maybe Alicia can help me back to my room and check my vitals." He shrugs. "Alastair said he would send her, but she hasn't been by."

Malachy glances at me. "Did Alastair tell you to check on Niall?"

I shake my head. "No, he must have forgotten." I stand from the couch, dying to get out of this room. "I'll check his vitals now."

Mal grabs my hand before I have the chance to escape. "Alicia, we need to talk about Sasha in more detail. It's not like you."

I reclaim my hand. "Drop it, Mal. You know I'm stressed, and I just flipped out."

Malachy's eyes flash when I call him Mal, but it's a habit I struggle to shake. "Fine, but now I've got to deal with Sasha and make sure she doesn't call the police and press charges." He loosens his tie, and I can see the weight of his position weighing heavily on him. "Another problem," he mutters.

I regret my actions the moment I see the stress it brings to my big brother. All my life all I've been is a burden to him. It's time I broke away and started taking responsibility for my actions. "No. Leave it to me. I made this mess, I'll sort it."

His brow furrows. "As her employer, I need to sort it out."

"It was an altercation between the two of us." I set my hand on his shoulder. "Please let me fix it."

He searches my eyes for a few seconds before conceding. "Fine. But please don't punch her again."

"Don't worry. I won't." I walk away to join Niall, who is watching me intently. "I'll talk to you later." I don't look back, feeling relief that I've escaped my brother's questioning.

Once we're out of earshot of Malachy, Niall leans toward me. "What the fuck happened, baby girl?"

I shake my head. "Sasha knows about us. She has pictures."

Niall stops and grabs my hand, forcing me to look at him. "She tried to blackmail you?" he asks, eyes full of that hot, passionate rage.

I nod. "Yes, she wants me to stop seeing you." I pull my hand from his. "Apparently you two were fucking a couple of months ago."

There's a flash of guilt in his eyes at the mention of their relationship. He shakes his head. "It was nothing, Alicia."

I'm not sure why he feels the need to justify it to me, especially since it was before anything happened between the two of us. "It has nothing to do with me, Niall. I'm just telling you what she said."

"Come on, we can talk about this in my room," he says, leading the way.

It's hard to believe how quickly he has recovered from his injuries, even though they aren't fully healed. It shows how tough he is that he's on his feet already.

Once we get to his room, he turns to face me. "Why did you punch her though?"

I narrow my eyes at him. "Because she was being a first-class bitch, trying to blackmail me with photos of us."

He runs a hand through his hair. "So, it wasn't because you found out I'd slept with her?"

"What are you accusing me of, Niall?"

He steps toward me, setting his hand on either side of my shoulder. "I'm trying to work out if you are as crazy about me as I am about you."

I feel my heart hammer harder in my chest. "Fine. I snapped when she told me you two had been fucking."

He smiles. "So jealous, little lass." He brushes a hair from my face and tucks it behind my ear. "I like it."

I shake my head. "It's not who I am. You are turning me into a psycho just like you."

Niall goes to the bed and lies down, making me wonder what he's doing. "Time to check my vitals, nurse." He slides his jogging pants down and his thick cock stands to attention.

A tightness ensues in my gut as white-hot lust spreads through my veins, taking my brain captive. "You are injured, Niall."

He stokes his cock, making my mouth water. "Hence why you are on top, baby girl. Make me feel better."

I shake my head. "Aren't we going to talk about the fact we need to tell Malachy before Sasha spills her guts?"

Niall growls in warning. "No talking, sit on it now before I come over there and force you against the wall."

It's crazy that his disrespectful, dominant ways

only feed the bonfire of desire blazing inside of me. "Yes, daddy," I say, walking over to him and unbuttoning my top.

Niall's eyes are intense and almost glow in the dim light of his room.

It's been over a week since we last had sex, and I've been going out of my mind. I drop my blouse to the floor and then unbutton my pants, slowly teasing him as I draw them down my body.

"Do you know what happens to naughty girls who tease?" Niall asks.

I bat my eyes at him innocently. "I don't know what you are talking about, daddy."

He wraps an arm around me and forces me onto the bed, spanking my ass hard.

The impact makes me yelp in surprise as I feel the hard length of him pressing hungrily against my abdomen.

"This is a bad idea while we're in the middle of a crisis," I say, unable to get my mind off of Sasha's threat.

Niall spanks my other cheek. "I don't want to hear any more about that jealous, spiteful bitch. I'll deal with her after I fuck you." Niall spanks me a few more times before speaking, "Now sit on my cock like a good girl."

I bite my lip and adjust myself to sit on his hard length, groaning the moment he slides through my dripping entrance. "It's been too long," I gasp, feeling utterly gone with desire. My body moves on its own accord, riding him like my life depends on it.

Niall grabs my hips, taking control, even though he should be resting. "I will always take care of you, Alicia. Do you understand?" he asks, his voice oddly serious considering what we're doing.

I meet his gaze. It feels like his eyes burn a hole right through my soul. "Yes, daddy. I understand."

He wraps a hand around the back of my neck and forces my mouth to his. There's something different about the way he kisses me; the passion is laced with a tenderness that makes my entire body ache.

I hate the way hope pools inside of me. Hope that perhaps I can have it all. Niall and the baby. All of us a family living happily ever after.

Life has been hard up to now, but it's taught me one thing. There's no such thing as happily ever after, especially not for people like us.

## 18

## NIALL

*I*'m going out of my mind with boredom.

Malachy is in Salem, trying to get one up on Milo. They are tracking the routes they take with their drug shipments, hoping to commandeer a large haul.

Aiden Henderson has stepped into my shoes. Perhaps I'll find I'm jobless once I get back on my feet, especially if Malachy finds out about his baby sister and me.

Alicia has been studying hard for her finals and out taking them this week, leaving me longing for her to return.

Neither of us has raised the glaring issue of Malachy and Sasha after that day. I intended to after Alastair discharged me from his care, but I couldn't find the right time to broach the subject.

A part of me wishes she would bring it up again. As I know that mentioning it means I'm declaring I want to be with her forever. Fear of rejection holds me back. Alicia wouldn't tell her brother about us unless she was all in.

I glance at the clock, noticing it's long past midnight. Alicia is normally here by now, and the fact she won't answer my calls is irritating me. She texted me to say she was meeting her friend Jane after her exam, but that was hours ago. Patience is not my forte with her.

The door swings open and she walks in, looking a little stressed.

"What time do you call this?" I ask, unable to suppress the anger in my tone.

She shrugs. "Jane and I had an enjoyable night in watching movies and eating Chinese."

Her nonchalance only makes me long to punish her, but first we have a matter to discuss.

"How did the exam go?" I ask.

She shakes her head. "It was fucking hard." She holds a hand to her forehead. "I think I flunked it."

I laugh. "That's what you said about the last one and you aced it. Don't be so hard on yourself, baby girl." I tap my palm on the bed, inviting her to sit. "Come sit with me."

Alicia does as I say, sitting on the side of the bed and placing her hand in mine. "How was your day?"

"Boring as hell, until now." I lace my fingers in her

hair and pull her mouth to mine, kissing her deeply. Anxiety twists at my gut at the mere thought of bringing up Malachy. "We need to talk, little lass."

She tenses slightly. "Talk about what?"

I search her emerald eyes, hoping that she feels the same way I do. "About our plan."

"What plan?" she asks.

"It's getting risky with multiple people knowing about us." I lace my fingers with hers and squeeze. "Do you think it's time we tell Malachy?"

Her eyes widen. "Are you insane? I thought you sorted the threat from Sasha."

I swallow hard, knowing that this is the reaction I feared. "I did, but it's better to come clean than to let someone else tell him."

Alicia reclaims her hand and stands, pacing away from the bed. "Do you realize what that would mean?"

As I stare at her, pacing up and down, my fears are becoming a reality. She's scared of this, of us. "It means that I'm serious about you."

When she turns around, tears fill her eyes. "I'm not sure you understand what that means, Niall."

My brow furrows. "It means I want to spend the rest of my life with you, that's what it means."

She shakes her head, folding her arms over her chest. "How can you be sure? We've been sleeping together for just under a month."

I laugh at that. "Yeah, and we've only known each

other for thirty years." There is no doubt in my mind that she is what I want forever.

Although I feared this reaction, deep down I didn't expect it. I thought we were both on the same page. "So you don't want this? Us?" I clarify.

Alicia looks torn as she stares at me with tears running down her cheeks. "I don't know what I want, Niall. I don't think you do either."

"Where is this coming from?" I can't understand why she is being this way, entirely closed off from the idea of telling her brother. "Is it because you fear he will kill me?"

Alicia turns her back to me, and it grates on my last nerve.

I swing my legs out of the bed and stand, pacing toward her. My injuries still ache but it's a dull pain I hardly notice anymore.

Alicia tenses as I set my hands on her shoulders. "Talk to me, baby girl. I only want to take care of you."

I brush her hair out of the way and press my lips to the back of her neck, feeling her instantly relax.

"Niall," she murmurs my name.

The need inside of me ignites despite her refusal to tell her brother about us. "I'll wait as long as you want to tell him, or never tell him. All I want is to make you happy, little lass." I force her to face me, feeling my chest ache at the tears streaming down her face. "What's wrong?" I wipe the tears away, pressing my forehead against hers.

"Nothing," she says, but it's a damn lie if ever I've heard one. I don't have the strength to argue with her about it right now; all I want to do is drown in her.

A hard knock at my door startles the both of us apart.

"Niall, open up," Calum calls.

"Shit," Alicia breathes.

I tighten my grip on her hips and kiss her softly. "Hide in the bathroom."

She nods and slips into the bathroom, locking the door.

I open the door. "What the fuck do you want at this time of night?"

"The Italians blew up the warehouse at the docks." He holds his hands up. "I thought you ought to know, lad."

"Fucking bastards. I assume Malachy has been informed?"

He nods. "Yeah, he's on his way down there."

"Okay, I'll get dressed. Can you drive me?"

Callum's brow furrows. "Aren't you supposed to be on bed rest?"

I crack my neck. "Malachy doesn't think clearly when he's under attack. I need to be there. Can you drive me?"

He nods. "Of course. I'll be out front with the car."

I clap him on the shoulder. "Thanks, see you in five." I shut the door.

Alicia comes out of hiding. "What are you thinking?"

"Mal needs me down at the docks." I approach her and wrap my arms around her waist. "I'll be okay, I promise."

She shakes her head, pushing me away. "Alastair's orders were clear. You need to stay in bed for another week at least. You aren't even better and you want to head straight into another war zone." The look in her eyes is one of pure disappointment.

"The police will be on the scene, Alicia. I'm not heading to a gang shoot out, for fuck's sake." I grab the back of her neck and pull her close, angling her face upward to me. "When I say I'll be okay, I mean it." I press my lips to hers, but she resists. I force my tongue into her mouth.

She finally submits, moaning as I claim her fully. My fingertips press into her hips hard, and it takes all my self-control to stop myself from fucking her. I break away from her. "I want you here when I get back, baby girl, wet and ready," I murmur before walking toward the closet to get dressed.

She doesn't say another word, watching me as I leave her. Part of me is thankful that Calum knocked on my door when he did. It saved me from the heartbreaking truth. Alicia isn't in this as wholeheartedly as

I am. If she were, she would have jumped at the idea of breaking this to Malachy and becoming official.

---

Calum waits in the car as I get out. "Don't stick around. I'll get an Uber back." His brow furrows. "Are you sure?"

I nod. "Yeah, best Mal doesn't know who told me, aye?"

Calum pales slightly but doesn't need to be told twice. He puts the car into reverse and turns around. I turn my attention to the utter chaos in front of me. Smoke billows hundreds of feet into the air above our warehouse building.

I notice a group of our guys, including Malachy, gathered at the entrance of one of our other warehouses. They are no doubt coming up with some kind of insane, dangerous plan. Luckily for them I have a better one since my injuries have me locked up in my room. I've been doing research and found our best opportunity to strike down Milo Mazzeo for good.

I march confidently over to the warehouse, sneaking up on the group of men who are quietly discussing their options.

"I heard about the explosion. The doctor has signed me off to come back," I lie, interrupting them. Alastair would kill me if he knew I was here.

Malachy turns around and smiles, walking toward me. "Welcome back, lad." He pulls me into a hug, clapping me on my back. I wince internally at the pain of my injuries, but don't let him see it. "I'm glad you're back in time for the most epic plan ever."

*Here we go.*

"What kind of plan?"

"We're going to take out Fabio's shipment before it even lands on American soil," he answers.

I knew they'd be coming up with something stupid, but this takes first price. "That's a bad fucking idea, Mal."

I notice Malachy grit his teeth. "For fuck's sake, you're back one minute and immediately blow the wind from my sails."

I laugh as, although it's true, he will thank me in the end. "You would start a war with Enzo D'Angelo and Fabio Alteri. Do you think we can fight a war against three Italian crime organizations?" Milo struck up a deal with the New York City Don a few weeks ago, giving him a new avenue to bring in his merchandise. We couldn't be sure whether we'd be intercepting Enzo's shipment or Milo's.

Malachy's shoulders visibly slump. "Not really, but how else can we strike back for this stupid fucking move?"

I smile. "It looks like I came back at the right time. There's a high-stakes casino night at Milo's casino in the center of the city tonight. All of his top men will be in attendance. I say let's blow it up and end this shit once and for all."

"What the hell would we do without you, Niall?" Malachy asks. I wonder if he would be so happy if he knew what I'd been doing with his baby sister for a month now.

I shrug. "End up in a war you can't win, it would seem."

Mal claps his hands together. "Okay, we run with Niall's plan as it's perfect." His brow furrows, and he pauses, looking at me. "How did you find out about the casino night?"

My informant on the inside is a secret to everyone. It was one stipulation when he agreed to feed me information. "I heard about the high-stakes casino night from an informant on the inside."

"Good work." Mal claps me on the shoulder, sending pain through my wounds again. "You best get in touch with Patrick and get the explosives we need fast, planting them there before tonight."

It feels good to be back, even if I shouldn't be yet. "On it, sir." I turn away and walk out of the warehouse, knowing that perhaps if I pull this off, it will be easier when we tell Malachy the truth.

Alicia may not have agreed yet, but she will. There is one thing she underestimated when we crossed the line with each other. I don't take no for an answer.

Alicia is in my blood and the only way she's

getting out of this is with my heart no longer beating. I don't think Alicia has it in her to kill me to escape me. Deep down, I know she wants this as much as I do, she's just scared of the consequences.

19

## ALICIA

*I*'m a mess of nerves as I wait for Niall to return, knowing that I've got to meet Scarlett for breakfast in less than an hour.

Last night I texted her and asked her if she wanted to hang out for the day, as it's about time that I got to know the girl that has captured my brother's icy heart.

Niall left for the docks hours ago, promising he would return and not get involved. My gut tells me he's back to work as usual, despite his injuries.

The door swings open, and he enters, a strained look on his face. "Hey, little lass." He shuts his eyes for a moment. "I bought you something."

My brow furrows as I notice he's holding a hand behind his back. "What is it?"

He raises a brow. "Come here and find out."

I hesitate, wondering what he's up to.

Once I get close, he pulls out a large red panda soft toy. "I know it's your favorite animal. I wanted to get you something."

Tears prickle my eyes as the closest thing I got to a stuffed toy as a kid was the pillow Niall gave me. At least, as far as I can remember.

I was so young when my parents died, I can't remember what I had back then. According to my shrink, she thinks I have selective memory from the trauma of their deaths and the shit that followed. Malachy insists that my childhood was a blissfully happy one until the crash, I just don't remember it.

I hug the panda and smile at him. "Thank you," I say, wrapping my arms around his neck and hugging him tightly, still holding the panda in one hand.

Niall has looked after me since we first met. We always made perfect fucking sense, so it's ridiculous it took me this long to realize it.

He growls softly. "I didn't hear the magic word, Alicia."

I bite my lip. "Thank you, daddy. I love it." I step away from him and hug the toy close, feeling safer than I've ever felt.

He groans and I notice him sway a little.

"Are you okay?" I ask, placing my hand on his arm.

He shakes his head. "Fuck, I think I overdid it."

The reminder that he went back to work despite being told he needed another week in bed snaps me back to reality. "You shouldn't have gone at all. Why were you so long?" I ask.

He slumps down on the bed, shutting his eyes. "Malachy thinks Alastair signed me off. He sent me on a few errands."

I clench my fists by my side. "I'll fucking kill that idiot."

Niall chuckles. "No, you won't. You will come and sit on my lap as I've got blue balls ever since I left you earlier."

I sigh heavily, wishing he wasn't so hard to resist. After the way we left things earlier, Niall's answer to it is to fuck rather than talk. I'm torn over what to do because of the baby. Before we tell Malachy, I need to come clean to Niall.

It's a tempting prospect to forget about it, but I know we shouldn't ignore the elephant in the room. "What about our conversation?"

His eyes flash with irritation. "Are you seriously going to bring that up right now?"

I grit my teeth. "There's no point brushing it under the carpet."

"Fine, you want to talk, then listen. I don't care if you say you don't want this for the long term because the moment you let me inside of you, you became mine, Alicia." He stands up, wincing as he does. "There is no world where escaping me is an option, do you understand?"

I back away from him, finding him both scary and

sexy when he gets like this. "No, I'm not some doll you can order around, Niall." I cross my arms over my chest. "If I decide I want out, then I'll get out."

His jaw clenches, and he continues to walk forward, backing me against the wall. "Is that right?" He teases his hand to my neck, squeezing hard. "Then why do you always break whenever I touch you?" He brings his lips to my ear and nibbles on it. "You want this. No matter how much you tell yourself it's just a fling. It's not."

My chest aches hearing him say that, as it's not a fling to me either. I just don't think he will want what is growing inside of me.

When I was about twenty years old, I remember the three of us discussing if we'd ever have children. Niall was adamant that he could never be a father. He doesn't want children, and I won't give up our child. That may have been eighteen years ago, but I doubt things have changed drastically since then.

It's the only thing holding me back from telling him the truth. Instead, I kiss him, knowing it's easier to forget my problems. It's easier to lose myself in the man I love more than anything in this world, except our unborn child.

If having our baby means I have to be without Niall, then so be it. Motherhood was something I never thought I'd get to experience as I got older. Now I'm pregnant, and I can't wait to be a mom.

Niall growls softly, lifting me against the wall. "I've been thinking about fucking you all morning."

"I haven't got long. Scarlett is meeting me for breakfast at nine."

He bites my collarbone hard enough to break the skin, making me groan. "I don't care. I'm going to take as long as I want with you." Niall carries me to the bed and sets me down gently, climbing over me.

I moan as he pulls open my nightdress and sucks on my stiff, sensitive nipples. His tongue lavishes attention on them with expert precision.

Every nerve in my body hums to life as his hands and mouth work me into a frenzy before he's really started.

Niall is an addiction. No matter how much of a dominant, possessive asshole he is, I still want him like my life depends on it.

"Fuck me," I breathe.

Niall stops and smiles at me. "I think you are forgetting the magic word again." He bites my bottom lip between his teeth. "Perhaps I need to punish you."

"I'm sorry. Please fuck me, daddy."

He groans, turning feral as he kisses a path down my stomach. "Not until I get a taste."

I tighten my fingers in the bedspread's fabric as his tongue slides through my soaking wet entrance. Niall is a fucking god. The things he does to me with his tongue should be illegal.

Before I know it, he has me panting and moaning

like a dirty slut. "Make me come, please," I cry, feeling myself on the edge of no return.

He stops and glances up at me, raising a brow. "Not until my cock is inside of you."

"Then what are you waiting for?" I ask, feeling every inch of my body tingle in anticipation.

Niall flips me onto my front forcefully and grabs something from under the bed.

"What are you doing?" I ask.

He doesn't answer me, fastening my wrists and ankles into the cuffs attached to his bed. Next, he places a blindfold over my eyes. The removal of one of my senses both scares and excites me.

I tense when I feel something cold and wet against by asshole. "What are you doing, Niall?"

"Relax, baby, I'm going to put a plug in your ass while I fuck you."

The idea scares me. I've never done anal play except by myself. Giving that kind of trust to another human being not to hurt me takes serious guts, but somehow I know I can trust Niall with anything.

His finger slides through my tight back hole suddenly. The lube makes it easy to accept and the fact that I trust this man with every thread of my soul. "That feels... good," I breathe as he gently works me open.

It's crazy that I can't see what kind of plug he's intending to use, or how big it is, but it makes the entire situation ten times more thrilling.

He adds another finger, stretching my hole the way no man ever has. I've trusted no one enough to go near that part of my body, but Niall owns every inch of me, and we both know it.

After a few blissful minutes of Niall stretching my ass, something larger and firmer nudges at my entrance. Instinct makes me tense.

"Relax, baby girl. I'd never hurt you." He adds more lube to my well stretched hole as I let go of the tension, handing him all the power.

The firm toy slips easily through the tight ring of muscles, filling me in a way nothing has ever filled me before. It's definitely larger than the little one I own.

"How does it feel?" Niall asks.

I swallow hard, getting used to the oddly pleasurable sensation of the size. "Good. It feels good," I say.

Niall's tongue dips into my dripping wet pussy as he tastes me. It feels better than ever with the plug in my ass and not being able to see. He takes everything from me and then gives me much more back.

"Oh God, I'm going to come," I cry, feeling my orgasm approaching faster than ever.

Niall stops while I'm on the edge, chuckling. "Fuck, you must love having your ass plugged to come that fast." He spanks my ass. "Are you ready to experience being stuffed in both holes at the same time?"

"Yes, daddy," I moan, feeling utterly gone right now.

The tip of his hard cock presses against my aching

pussy. Niall thrusts forward but slowly, allowing me to get used to the foreign sensation of the plug in my ass. I feel so full. It's both painful and pleasurable, as he works his cock back in and out again.

After a few thrusts, I feel my pussy loosening up. My body is accepting the invasion in both holes and loving it. He fucks me gently, easing me into it with a tenderness that shakes me to the core. Niall cares about me in ways no one ever has.

The sensation is so damn good I come quickly and with such vigor it knocks the air from my lungs.

Niall growls above me, coming undone a few strokes after me. I don't know how long we stay there in that position, basking in the afterglow of our sex. All I know is that I trust Niall with every damn part of my body. I just don't know if I can trust him with news that changes everything.

Niall finally pulls out of me, but he doesn't take the plug out. He unfastens the blindfold and restraints.

"Are you forgetting something?" I ask.

He spanks my ass. "No, little lass. It's good training to keep it in all day."

I turn over and stare at him in disbelief. "Are you serious?" The look on his face tells me he is.

"Be a good girl and do as I say." He kisses me. "Shower now, or you will be late."

*Shit.*

I totally forgot about breakfast. Ten minutes to

shower and dress. I get up and head for the bathroom, turning on the faucet. Niall joins me, washing my body with careful precision. His kisses make it almost impossible to leave the shower.

"Stop that, you are going to make me late."

He smirks. "Fine." He turns off the faucet and guides me out of the shower, drying me with my towel. "Let me dress you," he whispers into my ear.

The idea of him dressing me makes me feel so cherished. It's a hard feeling to put into words. Niall cares for me in ways I've longed for since I was a little girl.

I wait in the bedroom for him to pick an outfit. Since I've spent so much time in his room, I keep a lot of my clothes in here. He selects a classy navy blue halter neck top and white pants, dressing me in them.

I can't fault his choice. They look perfect together.

"Thank you, daddy," I say, running my hands over his bulging biceps. "Shall I dress you?"

He shakes his head. "No, baby girl. Watch me." He nods to the bed, and I sit down.

I watch as he dresses in a beautiful silk shirt and black pants. He doesn't opt for a tie today, but he shouldn't be working. He should come clean to Malachy that Alastair didn't clear him for work.

"Are you sure you should work in your condition?"

Niall finishes buttoning his shirt. "I'm fine. Stop

worrying." He grabs my hand and leads me out of his bedroom. Once we're in the corridor, he stops and pulls me against him. "Dinner tonight at your favorite place." It's not really a question, but a demand.

I nod in reply. "Sounds good."

"See you at The Three Amigos. Eight o'clock sharp," Niall murmurs, wrapping his arms around me.

"Yes, daddy," I reply, searching his lustful eyes.

He kisses me as though his life depends on it. The depth of emotion almost hurts as I kiss him back, knowing that tonight I have to tell him the truth.

The baby growing inside me complicates everything. Before I tell my brother about us, I need to know whether Niall wants this. The full package. A family of his own. If not, then Malachy will simply learn that I had a one-night stand with a stranger and wound up pregnant. He need never know about the two of us sneaking around behind his back.

Even though deep down I know this isn't the life he wanted. When he was twenty-three years old, he was so certain he'd never have children.

"Morning," Scarlett says, startling both of us.

We jump apart and guilt floods me that my brother's lover just caught us red-handed.

"Morning, Scarlett," I say, struggling to calm my firing heart. "Are you ready for breakfast?"

She nods in response. "Sure, is your friend joining

us?" She obviously doesn't know who Niall is, thank God.

Niall shakes his head. "No, I was just leaving." He exchanges a brief glance with me before turning and walking away.

Silence pulses between the two of us for a few moments as we watch after him.

"Who is that?" Scarlett asks.

I feel my gut twist. If anyone is going to get us caught, it will probably be Scarlett. She spends more time with my brother than anyone else. I shake my head "No one. Come on, let's get something to eat. I'm starving." Taking Scarlett's arm under mine, I lead her downstairs and toward the kitchen.

We've both gotten too careless lately. Kissing in the corridor is not a good idea. If we're not careful, everything could crash and burn before it has even truly started.

## 20

## NIALL

I walk down the familiar street, checking my watch. I'm five minutes late. Once I get to the corner where The Three Amigos is, I see her in her usual booth by the window. Her attention is fixed on the menu on the table. I can't help but smile the moment I set eyes on her.

This is the first time I've actually been to this restaurant, since I spent a lot of my time in the cafe opposite, watching her.

I walk past the window, tapping on it as I do.

Alicia smiles when she sees me, but it concerns me that the smile doesn't reach her eyes. She's nervous, but I don't know why.

I enter the restaurant and the hostess comes to greet me. "How can I help, sir? Have you got a booking?"

I shake my head. "My friend is already here." I point to the booth where Alicia is sitting.

She steps out of the way. "Of course, go ahead, sir."

I walk toward Alicia, feeling my heart pound hard in my chest. It always does whenever I'm near her. "Hey, little lass," I say, sitting down opposite.

While we're in public, I know better than to overstep the line, so I don't take her hand. Anyone who knows us could see us together here. Malachy doesn't need to hear about our affair from anyone but us.

"Hey," she replies, barely looking up from her menu.

I don't let it get to me, assuming she's preoccupied by her thoughts. "How was your day?"

Alicia continues to focus on her menu, even though I'm aware she orders the same thing every single time she comes here and has done for years. She doesn't need to look at the menu. "It was okay, how was yours?" she asks, meeting my gaze for the first time since I took my seat.

"It was good." A few moments of awkward silence pass between us. "Is it still in there, baby girl?" I murmur quietly, wondering if she would dare disobey me and take the plug out of her ass.

She shakes her head. "No, it was too uncomfortable."

I growl softly. "I'll have to punish you for that later."

Alicia doesn't reply, making me wonder what is up with her. "Are you okay?"

"Not exactly." She sighs. "I've got some news, but maybe we should get you a drink first." Alicia flags down the server. "Can I get a Budweiser and a glass of water, please?"

I wonder what the news could be. Perhaps she really did flunk her last exam for her PHD. It's the only reason I can think of for her being so down. The server nods and walks away, noting the order.

"Who is the water for?" I ask.

She shrugs. "I don't feel like drinking alcohol." She returns her attention to her menu, driving me crazy.

"Alicia," I growl her name, feeling agitation growing inside of me. "Look at me, now."

Her eyes meet mine, and the fear in them is heightened. I can't understand what she has to fear from me.

*What is she scared of?*

"You are acting weird. What is going on?" I shake my head. "You order the same thing in this restaurant every time and yet the menu seems to mesmerize you."

Alicia worries her bottom lip between her teeth, her eyes searching mine as if she's trying to find an answer to a question she has yet to ask me. The tension in the air heightens as she remains silent. The server returns to our table with my beer and her water, breaking the tension momentarily.

I press her once he walks away, "Alicia." I infuse the tone of my voice with warning.

Her eyes glisten with unshed tears. "I'm sorry, Niall." The tears shed down her cheeks.

It kills me to see her hurting like this. "Sorry for what, baby girl?" I question, reaching for her hand and squeezing. For a moment, I forget we're in public, where any of the clan's members could see us. We already have enough people aware of this relationship without anyone else discovering the truth. "Tell me what's wrong."

She pulls her hand away and crosses her arms over her chest. A few painful moments pass by before she speaks, "I'm pregnant, Niall."

Those words feel like a blow to the stomach. All the blood drains from my face as I stare at the woman in front of me, gobsmacked.

*Pregnant.*

Fear so acute slams into me, and I feel myself disappearing behind walls I thought I'd demolished a long time ago. Numbness spreads through every vein. I feel my emotions shutting down as the news shocks me to the very core. Out of all the words I expected her to say, pregnant was the last one. Perhaps it's foolish. We haven't been careful since we started sleeping together. It never occurred to me to check whether Alicia was on birth control.

It feels like she derailed my world with one simple word, as I know I can't be a father. Ever since I was young, I vowed I wouldn't have a family. All families do is hurt each other.

*How can I be a father when I never had one myself?*

I don't know the first thing about caring for a child.

"Say something," she says, tears streaming down her face.

*What can I say to such shocking news?*

"I don't know what to say, Alicia."

She nods and dries her eyes, sitting up straighter. "I knew it. This is a deal breaker for you, isn't it?"

I don't know. One minute I know without a doubt that I can't live with her, the next I feel like running the other direction. I shrug. "Do you want the baby?" It's a dick question, one that shouldn't even come out of my damn mouth.

Tears streak faster down her face as she stares at me in disbelief. "How can you ask me that?"

"Well, you've just finished your doctorate. A baby will hamper the career you want to pursue." I can tell my words are hurting her.

The flash of rage in her eyes is proof enough as she sits up straighter. "I will have this baby with or without you, Niall. I'll also become a doctor and land the job I want." She clenches her fists on the table. "Especially since Malachy is going to be my employer.

This isn't going to change anything. I knew this would be your reaction."

I hold my hands out defensively. "What? I haven't done anything."

"Exactly. You are sitting there acting like this has nothing to do with you. Well, it doesn't have to." Alicia stands and looks me in the eye. "Goodbye, Niall." She turns away and walks toward the exit of the restaurant.

Dread rocks through me as I watch her walk away, knowing that we can't end like this. Baby or no baby, losing her isn't an option. I chase after her into the street. "Alicia, wait," I call, running after her and grabbing her arm. "I'm in shock."

She yanks her arm from my grasp and turns to look me in the eye.

"Can't you give me some time to process this?" I ask.

Alicia clenches her jaw, remaining strong as always. "Niall, your initial reaction is all I need to make this decision."

"What decision?" I ask, wondering if she's serious about breaking this off. Surely this is just a fight and we'll be fine later.

"Don't make this harder than it needs to be." She shakes her head. "I remember your opinion when the three of us discussed if we would have kids when we were younger." She smiles, but it's a sad expression. "You didn't want a child then, and it's clear you don't want one now. Nothing is going to change overnight."

I remember the conversation she is talking about, and she's right. This kind of thing never changes. You either feel you can be a parent or you don't. It's that simple. Although it got a hell of a lot more complicated a few moments ago. It means losing the one thing that matters the most to me.

Alicia turns around and hurries down the street away from me without saying another word.

The possessive, dark side of me can't and won't let her go. I march after her, one step of mine equaling two of hers. Catching her up, I stop her in her tracks, blocking her with my body. "Listen to me, Alicia," I order, grabbing hold of her shoulders forcefully. "I want you forever." I shake my head. "Nothing is going to change the fact I love you."

Three words I never thought I'd say to any woman. Her eyes widen, as it's the first time I've told her how I feel, even though I've known it since before our first kiss. "We can figure this out, together." I try to pull her close, but she resists.

"No, we can't, Niall." The pain on her face mimics my own. "Love isn't enough. I can't force you into being a father, because you'll resent me." She pulls away from me and steps toward the curb, flagging down a cab. "You need to accept that we both want different things from life and that is okay." The cab stops, and she opens the door. Her beautiful emerald eyes meet mine and there's such pain in them. "I'm glad we sorted this out before we came clean to Malachy." She slips into the back of the cab and shuts the door, pressing down the lock.

"Alicia," I call her name, trying to open the door.

She watches me with tears in her eyes before turning to the driver and giving him instructions.

He drives away, leaving me staring after her with a dark hole in my chest. Darkness and rage infiltrate my body as I stand there, mulling over the conversation we just had.

Alicia is wrong. Love is everything. I know that death would be kinder than living without her and our baby in my life. I never wanted to be a father. Hell, I'm scared half to death about the mere thought of it. There is one thing I'm sure of, though, that Alicia will make the most amazing mother.

My reaction to the news was my defensive side trying to kick in, but I'd never resent her for wanting our baby. It makes me admire her even more than I already do. Her strength is one of her sexiest characteristics.

I can learn to be a father, even if the prospect freaks me out.

The cab turns the corner and out of my sight. I pull my cell phone out of my pocket and call her, desperate for her to listen to me. I want her, no matter what, baby or no baby.

If a family is what she wants, then I need to be the man to give it to her.

The dial tone sounds before it cuts to messaging.

"Shit," I growl, making a few pedestrians stop and stare at me.

I glare back at them, irritated by the entire situation.

*Alicia, this is what I want. You, me, and the baby. Please hear me out.*

I send the text to her, feeling frantic as my heart pounds furiously in my chest.

Alicia is a hardheaded woman. She has been since we were kids. I think she's being unreasonable to drop this on me and then hold me to my initial reaction.

All I can do is hope I haven't screwed things up beyond repair. Alicia is mine and nothing in this world will ever change that fact.

21

## ALICIA

The driver stops on the quaint, suburban street in front of Jane's cute little house. I have many happy memories with Jane and her husband here, before he died six years ago.

"Thanks. How much do I owe you?" I ask.

The driver glances in the rearview mirror. "Twenty bucks."

I pull a twenty-dollar bill out of my purse and hand it to him, before slipping out onto the sidewalk. All the houses in this street look like they're off of a postcard, with perfect manicured gardens outside of each and every one.

I didn't even tell Jane I was coming over, too flustered to think straight. The light on the front porch is on, which means she's home. I step up to the porch and ring the door, waiting for her to answer.

Jane appears at the door, eyes widening when she

sees me. "Hey, what are you doing here?" she asks, opening the door. The moment she notices my spoiled makeup and tear-stained cheeks, she asks, "Are you okay?"

"I'm so sorry to turn up like this without calling." I shake my head. "Niall flipped out about the baby." It feels like saying the words starts the floodgates again. He doesn't want what I want, which means I'm doing this alone

"Oh, honey." She pulls me into a tight hug. "I'm so sorry. Come inside and tell me what happened." She ushers me into her home. "Have a seat."

I slump down on her couch, unable to organize the thoughts rushing through my mind.

Jane sits next to me with her legs up on the couch, angled toward me. "What happened?"

I meet her gaze and sigh. "We went to dinner, and I told him, but his reaction wasn't good." I rest my head back and shut my eyes. "He doesn't want to be a father."

"He told you that?" she asks.

"He didn't have to say it. His first question was, do you want the baby?"

Jane winces. "Ow, that's got to hurt. What an asshole."

I nod. "Yeah, and now I'm hungry, angry, and upset."

Her brow furrows. "I thought you had dinner."

"No, stupidly I told him before we ate."

Jane laughs. "Luckily for you, I've got leftovers of my famous meatballs. Not to mention, Ben and Jerry's for dessert."

"You are the best." My brow furrows. "Are the kids out?"

She nods. "Yep, all grown up now and out with friends more often than they are here. That's why I have so much leftover food."

I follow her into the kitchen where she puts the stove back on to heat it up. My phone buzzes for about the fifteenth time since I left Niall on the sidewalk.

"Is that him?" Jane asks.

"Yes." I switch it off. "I'm not ready to speak to him."

She grabs a glass and pours me some coke. "Here, because you can't drink."

I smile and take it, sipping it. "I think I knew deep down this would be his reaction. That's why it took me so long to tell him."

Jane sits opposite me and sips her glass of wine. "Considering what he went through as a child, it's expected that he'd be a bit emotionally unavailable, isn't it?"

I sigh. "Yes, I can't imagine the horror he experienced. All I know is if he doesn't want to be a father, then I don't want to force him into it." My brow furrows. "He'll resent me, even if he thinks he won't."

Jane's brow furrows. "So that's it then? You two are officially over."

My chest aches at the word *over*. It's too finite. "I don't know." I rub my face in my hands. "I think I might get out of town for a few days. Clear my head."

"That sounds an awful lot like running away, Alicia."

I shrug. "Well, would you want to see the man you love walking around your home after you broke up?"

"Fair point." She takes a sip of her wine. "You can always crash with me."

I smile. "That's a kind offer, but I'm thinking of visiting my aunt in New York for the weekend. I'll get some retail therapy."

Jane rolls her eyes, as she knows how much I love to shop. "You are so lucky your family is rich."

"Why don't you come with? Your kids are teenagers now and never here."

Jane's expression turns wistful. "You know I'd love to, but it's Jack's birthday this weekend. The big one."

My eyes widen. "Wait, how old is he now?"

"Eighteen years old on Saturday. Can you believe it?" she asks.

I shake my head, as I really can't. When Jane lost Darren six years ago, he was a little shy twelve-year-old. "I'll bring him something back from New York." I sigh. "Where has the time gone?" I ask her.

"Who knows? Two years and Ellie will be eighteen too." Tears well in her eyes. "They will fly the nest off to college, leaving me here as the sad widow alone for the rest of her life."

I grab her hand and squeeze. "It doesn't have to be that way, you know that."

Jane forces a smile, but it doesn't reach her eyes. "I know. I just can't let go of Darren. How can I find someone else?"

"I didn't necessarily mean dating. You can get out there and do things you want to do. Didn't you always want to take up yoga?"

Jane raises a brow. "I did until I became a single mother." She downs the rest of her wine. "Would you come with me?"

I laugh. "I am literally the least flexible person ever, but for you, I'll give it a shot."

"Thank you." Jane smiles. "Your food is ready." She turns off the stove and dishes me up a bowl of her famous spaghetti and meatballs. My stomach rumbles in anticipation.

I dig into the food as Jane talks about her kids. I try to focus on what she's saying, but my mind constantly drifts back to Niall.

The pure fear in his eyes when I said the word pregnant warned me of what was to come. He doesn't want to be a father. After I walked out of that restaurant, he would say anything to get me to stay.

"Do you want to watch a movie?" Jane asks, breaking me from my daze.

"Sure, what did you have in mind?"

Jane shrugs. "We can pick one out on Netflix."

I nod. "Sounds good." I grab my dish and put it in the dishwasher. "As long as there is Ben and Jerry's too." I glance at Jane.

She holds the tub up she already retrieved from the freezer. "Great minds think alike."

We settle down under a blanket on the sofa and choose a chick flick, eating the ice cream. Jane is always into the lighter movies. I love action and psychological thrillers, but right now, something lighthearted is what I need.

Although, it seems to be impossible to keep my mind off of Niall. No matter how hard I try, he's taken my brain captive like the rest of me.

---

The train rumbles into Grand Central station.

Malachy hasn't texted me back, but I know I had to tell him where I am or he'd freak out.

Aunt Elsie has lived in New York ever since she got divorced from our Uncle Darragh. If you ask me, it was the best damn decision she ever made to get rid of that waste of space. For some unknown reason, Malachy insists on supporting his family. Family that never helped us in our time of need.

Elsie has always been lovely to us, she just didn't have the resources to help us when we went into foster care. Darragh was the one that refused, not her.

The station is packed as it so often is as I force my way through the crowd. The buzz of my cell phone catches my attention and I dig it out of my bag. Malachy is calling me.

"Hey, what's up?" I ask.

There are a few moments of silence. "What are you thinking going to fucking New York City?" he growls.

"Wow, calm down. I wanted a break from Boston. What's the problem?"

"We are at war with the Italians, Alicia. Italians that have a tentative alliance with Enzo D'Angelo. The mob boss in New York City."

I sigh heavily. "How the fuck am I supposed to know that, Mal? You never tell me anything." I shake my head in disbelief. "What has it got to do with me, anyway?"

"It's not safe for you to be roaming around his territory. You get to Elsie's, and you don't leave that apartment. I'm sending a car to get you."

My brow furrows. "You are being way too dramatic. I am not coming back to Boston."

There's a few moments of silence. "Alicia. This isn't some stupid game. If anyone there recognizes you—"

"Mal, this is New York City for fuck's sake.

There's millions of people living here, and you think they will notice me?"

There are a few moments of silence. "Fine, but you better be careful. If anything seems amiss you ring me right away. You got it?"

It's beyond belief that he's being like this. "Got it." I cancel the call.

Malachy may fear the Italians, but I've got nothing to do with whatever shit he's embroiled in. They can all leave me out of it.

I get out of the station and head for Fifth Avenue where my aunt lives in a stunning apartment with her husband, Grant. The walk is about thirty minutes, but I love it as I get to immerse myself in the bustle of New York. There's no city like it in the world.

My phone rings again, and this time it's Niall. I can't deal with talking to him this weekend. This time away from Boston is a chance for me to clear my head.

I type a text to him.

*Don't call me this weekend. I'm having time to myself.*

I send it, knowing he will be pissed with me. Niall isn't exactly good at taking instructions. I walk past St Patrick's Cathedral, stopping a moment to admire the beautiful architecture. Boston is my home and has been all my life, but if there is one place I would prefer to live, it's New York.

When I turn around to carry on walking, I bump straight into a guy. "Oh, sorry. I didn't see you there."

He smirks at me. "Don't mention it."

I move around him but can't understand why I feel dizzy. When I glance back, the guy has disappeared. I shake it off and try to ignore the odd sensation sweeping over my body.

Every step I take feels harder as my head starts to swim. I notice a bench up ahead with a guy sitting on it and sit next to him.

*What the hell is wrong with me?*

"Shit, I don't feel too well." I glance at the man next to me, wondering if I'm hallucinating as he smirks at me knowingly.

"Hello, Alicia. So kind of you to visit my city." The American-Italian accent is unmistakable.

"Who are you? What have you done to me?" I ask, trying to stand but finding my legs won't work.

"Enzo D'Angelo. Your brother was right; you made a big mistake coming here."

*How can he know what Malachy said to me?*

They must be monitoring Malachy's calls. A desperate need to warn him sweeps over me, but I know I can't. They've caught me in their city and now they're going to use me to their advantage.

Two men appear behind me, one of them being the man I crashed into a moment ago. Enzo speaks to them in Italian as I struggle to retain a grip of the threads of consciousness.

All I can think about in that moment is my baby. If they drugged me, what could it do to our unborn child. My world feels like it's spinning as everything becomes unfocused. I feel someone grab hold of me, but I have no strength to fight.

Malachy was right. Coming to New York City was a terrible idea.

22

# NIALL

It's Tuesday morning and Alicia still isn't home.

When I enquired about her whereabouts, Malachy said she'd gone to stay with their aunt in New York for the weekend. He said she would be back yesterday morning.

*I'm going out of my mind.*

New York was literally the worst place she could have visited, considering we're at war with the Italians. I drive toward Malachy's office block, knowing I have to come clean. She ran away because of me.

I pull into the underground parking lot and get out, heading for the elevator. Malachy might kill me when I tell him, but I can't stand by while Alicia might be in danger.

Her phone has been off ever since Sunday afternoon. It doesn't make any sense.

I get into the elevator and select the top floor, tapping my foot as it rises. The irritating elevator music only serves to incite the chaotic nerves building inside of me. Malachy seriously could kill me if he takes the news about us badly. Alicia insists we're over which perhaps means I shouldn't tell him. However, I'm done lying and sneaking around.

Whether or not she wants me, I'm coming clean and finding out why she's gone missing. The elevator opens and I step out.

The door to Malachy's office is open, meaning he's available. After the shit that went down Thursday night at Milo's casino, I'm surprised he's here at all. The Italians will be out for blood after foiling our plot to blow them away. Alicia might be held captive by them. It's all I can think ever since her phone stopped ringing on Sunday

I guess you can call me a dick for not respecting her boundaries, but I didn't call Friday or Saturday. Sunday I snapped only to find her phone went straight to voicemail.

I knock on his door. "I need to speak with you, Malachy."

He looks up from his computer. "You sound serious. What's up, lad?"

"Can I sit?" I ask, feeling the fear take hold. My best friend is certifiably insane and after the terrible week he had last week, my news isn't going to be welcome.

"Sure."

I sit down opposite him, trying to quiet my mind. *Where the hell do I start?*

"Well, spit it out, lad. I haven't got all day."

I draw in a deep breath. "I have something to admit. Something you won't like."

He raises a brow. "What?"

I may as well rip off the damn Band-Aid. "Alicia and I are sleeping together."

The rage that ignites in Malachy's eyes is a warning. He stands, bunching his fists by his side as he takes in the news. "Tell me that you are fucking joking."

I stand and back away from the desk, holding my hands up in surrender. "No, but before you lose your shit. It's serious, not a fling." That doesn't ease his rage as he steps around the desk, ready to fight. "She ran off to New York because we had a disagreement." I push myself to my feet, knowing that I need to be on high alert.

I've seen the look he has in his eyes too many times when he's in the ring. Malachy wants blood. He charges toward me with all his muscles clenched.

I read him well, knowing Malachy like no one else does. As his fist comes toward my face, I duck and swivel out of his path.

He growls and comes at me again. The enclosed space of his office plays to his strength, so I duck out of it and force him to chase me into the open plan lobby outside. "Coward," he shouts, glaring at me. "Face me like a fucking man, Niall." As I stare at my best friend, I'm painfully aware that he has the capacity to kill me with his bare hands. Especially since I'm still healing from my wounds.

I step away from him slowly. "Malachy, listen. I love her," I say.

He darts toward me fast, growling as he lands a punch against my jaw.

I wince at the pain radiating through me. The jolt alone was enough force to bring a healthy man to his knees. "Fuck," I say, stumbling over. If I was one hundred percent right now, it wouldn't have hurt so bad. "I'm still injured, Malachy." I force myself onto my feet before he can kick me while I'm down.

I bring my arms up to fend off his next punch. "I'd never hurt her. You know me."

Malachy stops and glares at me. "How long?"

I run a hand across the back of my neck. "It started the night you purchased your virgin, Scarlett."

He shakes his head. "Both of you have been sneaking around behind my back for over a month." There's not only rage in his expression but hurt. "Give me one good reason why I shouldn't kill you, Niall."

I swallow hard, knowing the only good reason. "Alicia is pregnant."

Malachy stares at me for a long while, frozen to the spot. "You got my baby sister pregnant?"

"Malachy, you're not listening to me." I hold my hands up. "I love her, and I'm telling you because I think she's in danger."

His eyes narrow. "Why do you think she's in danger?"

"You told me she was due back yesterday morning and her phone has been switched off since Sunday."

"There's one way to find out." Malachy picks up his office phone and calls someone. "Hey Elsie, is Alicia with you?"

The look on his face speaks volumes. Alicia isn't with her.

The blood drains from my face as I stare at my best friend, knowing that I may well have put her in serious danger by being a stupid, cowardly asshole.

"Okay, thank you." He cancels the call. "Alicia never made it to hers and texted her to say she had a change of plans." Malachy shakes his head. "A fact I know to be bullshit since I spoke to her when she got off the train at Grand Central Station."

"The Italians?" I ask.

He nods. "It has to be, but the question is how could they have known she was there before she even made it to Elsie's?"

We both stare at each other, racking our brains for the answer.

"Is your cell bugged?" I ask, believing it to be the only possible explanation.

Malachy's eyes flash with anger as he pulls his cell

phone out. I watch as he pulls off the battery cover in search of a bug. We both see it instantly and Malachy growls, "Motherfuckers," throwing the cell phone against the wall so hard it smashes into pieces. "One of those fucking Italians must have planted it on me at the casino."

A panic grips hold of me. "Does this mean that they have Alicia?"

Malachy runs a hand through his beard. "If they do, then they haven't played their hand yet." His brow furrows as he returns to the other side of his desk, sitting down in front of his computer.

"Why would they hold her captive but not say anything?" I ask.

Mal just shakes his head in reply.

"If we are right and the Italians intercepted her on the way to Elsie's then they've had her since Friday." I pace the floor. "it's Tuesday now. They could have done anything to her."

Malachy slams his hand onto the desk, hard. "I don't want to hear that, Niall. You say you love her, then go and fucking find her and bring her home."

I meet my best friend's gaze. "I will, but first I need some kind of lead." All I want to do right now is find her.

"What about your contact that gave you the intel on the casino night?"

That would work if he wasn't ghosting me after

what happened. "The incident spooked him. He won't speak to me."

"Fuck," Malachy says.

His computer dings, and I watch as Malachy's expression turns from curiosity to savage rage. "I will skin that Italian snake alive."

"What is it?" I ask, walking to the other side of his desk. My heart stops beating for a few moments. In that instant it feels like someone has shoved their hand into my gut and ripped out the contents.

The image on Malachy's computer is Alicia gagged and tied to a bed with Enzo D'Angelo standing one side and Milo on the other. They have a knife to her throat. I can't even find the words to express the emotions that hit me all at once.

Panic. Rage. Shock. The worst one is the soul crushing fear.

My entire body shakes as I stare at her fearful, wide eyes. They will not take my world from me.

"I will kill each and every one of them if they lay a hand on her, so help me God," I say, surprised at how calm my voice is compared to the chaos inside.

Malachy stands. "We will, brother." He holds out a hand to me and I take it. "You better marry my fucking sister once we get her back from them."

I look him in the eye. "I will." There is more conviction in those two words than any I've ever said. My reaction to finding out Alicia was pregnant was born out of fear, but any fear I've felt pales in comparison to the thought of losing her and our baby. "What's the plan?"

The smirk Malachy gives me is unnerving. "The Italians are smart, I'll give them that, but not smart enough." He points at something on the wall in the room where Alicia is kept.

My brow furrows as I try to read it. "What is that?"

"Fucking directions to where they are keeping her." He taps on his computer to enlarge the image.

It's a signed poster of The Rolling Stones, but I still have no idea where that is. "Sorry, lad, I don't know what that means."

He claps me on the shoulder. "They have her in the back room of Carnegie Hall in New York City. I read it's shut for refurbishment, so they obviously broke in thinking we'd never find her." He laughs. "Idiots didn't realize I've been in that exact room before."

Some of the tension eases hearing that we know where she is, but it's not good news. New York City is Enzo D'Angelo's territory. The moment we step foot on his turf, we're picking a fight with his organization.

"We could cause a bigger war than we are already fighting," I murmur.

Malachy shakes his head. "No, D'Angelo caused the war the moment he took my sister." The look in his eyes is one of gritty determination. "We better go and get her back, aye?"

"Let's do this," I reply, knowing that there is no other option.

Alicia is at the mercy of men that don't care whether she lives or dies. Our baby is in danger as well.

I made a mistake when I acted like a coward the moment she told me she was pregnant.

Now it's time to right that wrong.

23

## ALICIA

*Three days earlier...*

Hushed voices speaking a foreign language quickly replace the ringing in my ears. I try to roll over, only to find my arms and legs strapped down to the bed I'm lying on.

That's when my memories hit me like a barge train. The man on the bench who knew who I was.

*Enzo D'Angelo.*

I glance around the room, finding nothing familiar at all.

"Fuck," I mutter, trying to pull my arms from the tight restraints.

Panic coils through me as I wonder what kind of drug they gave me and whether it could harm my baby. These men care about nothing but money and power. Killing an innocent baby wouldn't faze them.

"Help," I cry, franticly trying to rip my arms from the restraints.

The door to the room I'm held captive in opens and two men enter, one of them is Enzo. "There's really no need for all that, Alicia." Enzo steps closer. "As long as your brother does as he's told, you will get out of here alive."

I glance at the other man, who has yet to say a word. His dark brown eyes chill me to the core. "Who are you?"

He smirks. "I'm a little offended you have to ask to be honest."

Enzo nods. "Yeah, have you been living under a damn rock?"

I guess I might as well have been. Malachy keeps me shielded from all the awful stuff that happens in his life. As a result, I'm ignorant to the world I belong to.

"My name is Milo. Milo Mazzeo."

The blood drains from my face as I stare at my brother's enemy. The man he's currently embroiled in a war with.

"Enzo was kind enough to lend his help since the war has got too far out of hand." He steps toward me and grabs a fistful of my hair hard, making me yelp. "Your brother has been a thorn in my side for too long now. I'm going to end it once and for all." He tilts his head. "Did you know he tried to blow my casino up with my wife and me in it only last week?"

*For fuck's sake, Malachy.*

I wish that he would put his ego aside and accept a truce. The bloodshed isn't worth it. All because of a damn car. At least, that's how it all started as far as I'm aware. "Why are you both fighting over a car?"

Milo releases my hair and his brow pulls together. "This didn't start with his car. I killed your cousin unwittingly because he was stealing from me for the Russians."

Malachy told me Dillion died in a car crash. There was never any mention of him being killed by his enemy. "That's news to me." I feel embarrassed that I don't even know how my cousin died. Darragh even lied to my face, saying that Dillion crashed as well. It feels like all my family have ever done is lie to me.

Enzo and Milo laugh. "Sounds like Malachy keeps you on a shorter leash than I ever imagined," Milo says.

He nods at Enzo, who draws a large, serrated blade out of a holster at his waist.

"Now it's time to make your brother sweat," Milo says.

I swallow hard, trying to still the horror sweeping through me. "Please don't hurt me."

Milo's dark, cruel gaze burns into me. "That all depends on your brother, sweetheart. You better pray he loves you enough to submit to my demands."

Malachy loves me, but he also loves his reputation.

He's crazy enough to try to refuse Milo's demands and find another way to get me back. I know him better than anyone, and his answer is never to back down, even if it might get me killed.

"Where am I?" I ask.

Milo folds his arms over his chest. "You are still in New York City. Somewhere your brother will never find you."

Enzo presses the knife against my throat, making me tense. "Now, smile for the camera." Another man I hadn't noticed stands in the doorway holding a camera.

I keep still in utter shock as the two men pose for the picture.

Once done, they release me.

I grab hold of my throat, making sure it's not cut. The phantom press of the serrated blade feels present against my skin. "What the hell was that?"

Enzo grabs the camera from the man and pulls up the photo on the small screen. "Photographic evidence that we have you. We are going to wait a few days until we send it, make him sweat."

Little does he know that Malachy isn't expecting me back until Monday morning anyway.

Milo nods. "Sit tight. Hopefully your brother will do the right thing."

I don't know why I ask this next question. "And, if he doesn't?"

The glint in Milo's eyes is so dark and twisted it

sends ice flowing through my veins. "I will enjoy sending you back to him piece by piece." He turns his back on me and walks away, followed by Enzo. They slam the door behind them, making me jump.

Pain clutches at my chest as I wonder what I did to deserve this. I always knew the clan's business was dangerous, but all my life, Malachy has kept me shielded from it. The same way he shielded me from the horrific parts of our childhood. Right now, I wish he hadn't, as I am not prepared for what is to come.

I hear footsteps coming toward the door and hold my breath, waiting for more intimidation.

Instead, the door opens and a very young and beautiful woman enters with a tray of food. "I thought you'd be hungry." She shuts the door quietly. "Don't tell anyone I brought you food though."

I smile at her kindness. "Not sure I'll be eating any though." I glance at my restrained arms.

She sets the tray down on a small table and then undoes the restraints around my wrists. "There, just so you can eat."

"Thank you." I take the tray, feeling my stomach rumble. "It's very kind of you."

She sits down in the chair next to me. "I have to be kind as you will not find any kindness from my husband."

I stop as I'm about to take a bite of the burger, meeting her gaze. "Husband?"

She tilts her head slightly. "Yes, I'm Aida Mazzeo."

My stomach churns and I place the burger down, unsure about taking anything from a woman married to that poor excuse of a man. "He said he would chop me into little pieces and send them to my brother."

She doesn't react, seemingly unsurprised by learning this. "Unfortunately, my husband is a very cruel man. Believe me, I've experienced it firsthand." She sighs heavily. "He's also desperate to end the war with your brother."

I nod in reply. "Malachy wants an end to it as well, but he's too stubborn and self-assured to accept defeat."

Aida laughs. "Same as my husband. Eat your food, I promise it's not poisoned or anything."

I glance between her and the burger, feeling confident that she has no intent to harm me. "Fair enough." I take a bite. "That is a good burger."

"Best in New York City. Believe me." She twirls her hair around her finger. "Vegetarian too."

I raise a brow and glance at the meat-like patty. "No way!"

She nods. "Yeah, I'm vegetarian and I wouldn't buy you meat, sorry."

"No need to apologize, it's really good." I finish the burger and eat some of the fries before speaking again, "Why are you being so nice to me?"

Aida looks uncertain about answering the question. "The truth is I've been where you are right now, although it was worse. I know how terrifying it can be."

"Really? Who kidnapped you?" I ask.

"Your brother, and I have the scars to prove it." She pulls down the collar of her shirt where three scars are visible.

"Goddamn it, Malachy," I murmur, irritated at my brother's clear lack of self-control over the darkness that rules him. "I'm sorry, my brother is sick."

"It wasn't your fault. Milo still holds it against him though." She purses her lips together thoughtfully. "Wouldn't the world be much more peaceful if only us girls were in charge?" She asks, a strange glint in her eyes.

"Yeah, like that would ever happen."

Aida sits up straighter and grabs my wrist, startling me. "What if we try to agree to a truce on their behalf?"

I shake my head. "Unfortunately, I'm the last person Malachy listens to."

"What about this woman he is with? Scarlett." she asks.

I sigh heavily, unsure exactly what Scarlett is to Malachy. It's clear he has an obsession with her. If it is a meaningful relationship remains to be seen. "I don't know. I can talk with her."

She nods. "Yes, try to. Once you are safe and away from here, we can arrange a meeting."

The idea of getting involved in this anymore than I already am scares me. "There's too much risk," I say.

Aida looks dejected. "What risk if we can save the men we care about from killing each other?"

I set my hand on my stomach. "I'm pregnant. Something I thought I was past but clearly not."

Aida's eyes widen. "Oh God, don't let Milo know."

I don't ask her why, as I feel her sadistic husband would use it against me. Instead, I just nod. "Let me think about it and talk to Scarlett. If I get out of this alive."

She squeezes my hand. "You will get out of this alive. I'll make sure of it. You and your baby."

I squeeze her hand back, thankful for her kindness during such a fearful ordeal.

It is rare you find someone like her in any walk of life, let alone when you've been kidnapped by her criminal mastermind of a husband.

She takes the tray, restores the restraints, and leaves without another word, allowing me to ponder her proposal alone. It is a tempting suggestion to stop the war dead in its tracks, however I wouldn't know the first thing about it and neither would Scarlett.

I think Aida is unaware that Scarlett knows nothing about this world Malachy dragged her into.

24

# NIALL

*A* tension you could slice through with a knife cloaks the ride to New York City. Malachy and I may have made a tentative truce in agreeing to save Alicia together, but I can tell he's pissed.

"Do you want to talk about it, Mal?"

He growls. "You know I hate being called Mal." His knuckles turn white as he takes the exit toward the city center.

"Sorry." I rub a hand across the back of my neck. "I just don't want this to come between us."

He glares at me before returning his gaze to the road. "We'll see about that once I hear Alicia's side of the story."

I narrow my eyes at my friend. "What are you suggesting?"

"Nothing, just shut up and let me drive." He indicates off the highway toward the city center. We don't really have a concrete plan. Neither of us are thinking straight because Alicia's life is in danger.

I cross my arms over my chest and look out of the window as the concrete jungle rushes by. Malachy will come around eventually. He may be a slave to his rage, but he wouldn't leave Alicia's baby fatherless. The rest of the journey to Carnegie Hall is silent as the burden of what we have to do rests heavily in the air.

Enzo D'Angelo is more powerful than Milo. It means we're taking on two gangs rather than one. An intimidating prospect, especially when we can't rely on any allies here in New York City. Devlin Murphy looks out for one person and that is himself.

There's a serious risk taking the fight onto another organization's turf, but Milo has left us with no choice. After what Mal did to his wife, I can only imagine the terrible things he will do to Alicia.

She's strong though. Stronger than anyone I know.

Malachy clears his throat. "Why did you and my sister have a disagreement?"

The question surprises me as I glance over at him. "I acted like a dick when she told me she was pregnant." I shake my head. "I was just in shock."

He runs a hand through his hair. "You better look after her and that baby once we save her. Or I really will kill you."

It's all I want. To be with Alicia and give her the

life she's always dreamed of. I remember the conversation she's talking about when we were in our twenties. She was insistent she wanted to be a mom. It's why I'm so surprised she never settled down, but Malachy has a lot of blame for that.

A selfish part of me was glad that he kept the men away all these years, despite knowing I didn't want the same things she did.

"Always," I reply.

Malachy takes a left at the lights and pulls up just opposite Carnegie Hall. "We need to stake it out before attempting to go in there."

My brow furrows as the longer we wait, the more damage they can do to her. "How long?"

He meets my gaze. "We can't fuck this up, Niall. We will only get one chance, and while I know you want to go in guns blazing, it's too dangerous."

Malachy isn't normally the one who speaks reason, but I guess he has to today because I am not thinking rationally. "You're right." I rub a hand across the back of my neck. "Since when are you the one thinking straight?"

He laughs. "Since the woman you love is in that building; love makes you irrational." His brow furrows. "I love my sister, but it's a different type of love." His Adam's apple bobs. "When Milo had his hands on Scarlett at the casino, I've never been so scared, Niall."

I can't believe my best friend has found love.

Maybe that's why he's calmer than I expected about the entire situation. "You love her, aye?"

He nods. "Yeah, she's pregnant too, Niall."

I raise a brow. "So the two best friends who both insisted they didn't want kids are about to become fathers?" I laugh.

Malachy's brow furrows. "You mean that conversation the three of us had?"

"Yeah, Alicia mentioned it when we argued. I had forgotten all about it, to be honest."

Someone exiting the hall from a side exit catches my attention and I elbow Malachy. "Who is that?"

He follows my gaze and claps his hands. "Aida Mazzeo." He reaches for the door handle. "Let's have a chat with her."

"Is that wise?" I ask.

He meets my gaze. "She let Scarlett and me escape the casino. Something tells me we can trust her to help us."

I glance between my friend and the woman, who is slowly disappearing further down the street. "Fuck it, let's do it."

We get out of the car and march after her, trying to catch her up. I'm surprised her husband allows her to walk around New York City without a bodyguard.

She turns left at the end of the street, and we follow into a quieter road.

"What if this is a trap?" I murmur to Malachy.

He shakes his head. "I doubt it."

"Aida," he calls her name once we're not too far from her.

She freezes, body turning stiffer than stone. Slowly, she turns around to face us. "Stay away from me, Malachy."

He steps forward, making her take two steps back. "Come now, lass, I only want to talk."

Aida's expression is fearful, which isn't surprising after the way he treated her. "You want Alicia, right?"

He nods. "Yes, can you help?"

"Why would I help you after what you did to me?" she asks.

Malachy holds his hands up. "Look, I was a royal asshole cutting you the way I did and for that, I'm sorry."

It's rare that I hear him apologize to anyone.

Aida's throat bobs as her attention darts between Malachy and me.

"The fact is, I got caught up in the idea of beating Milo any way possible." He shakes his head. "But, taking my sister and getting Enzo involved is a step too far in the wrong direction, if you ask me."

Aida nods. "I agree. That's why I snuck out to get Alicia something to eat." She shrugs. "I've been looking after her."

As I stare at the terribly young wife of Milo Mazzeo, a sense of pride hits me despite not knowing her. One look in her eyes and I can see she is above all this shit. She truly cares for people. Maybe Malachy was right that she might help us out. "How is she?"

Aida's eyes meet mine, and she smiles. "Niall, I assume? She's good." Her eyes move to Malachy. "Far better than I was as your captive."

"Can you help us out or not?" Malachy asks, cutting straight to the point.

Aida sighs and wraps her arms around her. "Milo would kill me if he found out I helped you."

Malachy shakes his head. "I don't think so. That man loves you. I saw it in his eyes when he came to rescue you."

"Not literally, but..." she trails off before nodding her head. "Fine, but all I will do is give you an in. After that, you are on your own." She approaches us, trusting we don't intend to hurt her. "All I want is for this war to end. Try to find a way Malachy." She sets her hand on his arm. "Promise me you will at least try?"

Malachy's jaw clenches, but he nods. "I promise, lass."

"Good." She releases his arm. "The door you saw me come out of, I'll keep it unlocked, but don't follow me straight in there." She runs her fingertips through her long, dark hair. "Milo and Enzo are out and won't be back until nightfall. It should give you enough time to flee the city." Her brow furrows. "I'll take back Alicia's food and give it ten minutes to come and get her. I have to remove her restraints so she can eat. If all goes to plan, it will look like I fucked up and forgot to lock the doors."

"Sounds good," I say.

"When you get inside, you go to the end of the corridor and turn right. Then along the next corridor and turn left. They hold Alicia in the second room on the right." Aida's brow furrows. "I'll carry on alone and get her food. You wait for me to return to Carnegie Hall." She turns to walk away and then stops. "By the way, how did you find out where she was?"

Malachy smiles. "Your husband isn't as smart as he thinks he is. The photo he sent was a giveaway."

Her brow furrows, but she doesn't question any further. "Stick to the plan." She walks off down the street.

I can't deny that I'm nervous about trusting the wife of our enemy. "Are you sure we can trust her?" I ask.

Malachy shrugs. "She's the best chance we've got. I think she is telling the truth. She wants an end to the bloodshed."

We walk back to the car and wait nervously, silence cloaking us.

"Did you mean what you said to her?" I ask.

"Which part?"

"That you promise to find an end to the bloodshed."

Malachy grits his teeth. "I will try, but it won't be easy."

He means he doesn't want to be the one to submit to a truce. The biggest problem with people like Malachy and Milo is that their egos are too fucking big. "You won't agree to a truce, then?"

"Let's focus on getting Alicia out alive, first." He sits up. "There she is." He glances at his watch. "Ten minutes until show time."

Aida walks to the same door, carrying a takeout bag. Her eyes dart around as if in search of us, but she doesn't see us parked across the street.

"What if she rang Milo to warn him we are here?" I ask.

Malachy shrugs. "Then we have to fight."

Hopefully, it won't come to that. I glance at my watch, counting down the minutes until I can rescue the love of my life. All I want is for all three of us to make it out alive, and then we can figure everything out from there.

Malachy hasn't killed me after I came clean, and that's a good sign. If he was going to, he would have done it by now.

"Show time," Malachy says, as the clock on the dash turns to eleven minutes past one o'clock.

"Let's do it." I get out of the car, trying to dampen down the warning bells ringing in my head.

We are about to walk into the devil's lair. Aida may or may not be telling the truth, but death is possible if we encounter either or both of the Italian Dons. Enzo is as ruthless as Milo if the rumors are to be believed.

All that matters is getting Alicia and our baby out of that building alive. If I have to sacrifice my life to achieve that, then so be it. I'd die for her a hundred times over.

## 25

## ALICIA

Milo returns to my room for the second time since I arrived here. Apparently, it's Tuesday, according to Aida. She just went to get me some food, which means if she returns too soon, Milo will find out she's been looking after me this entire time.

Milo approaches me, holding a gun in one hand. I try not to let him know how scared I am, as he strikes me as a man who thrives off other people's terror.

"It would appear your brother doesn't love you as much as I thought." He raises a brow. "Twenty-four hours since I sent him the photo and no response."

I hold my chin high. "That means nothing."

He presses the gun to the side of my head, spreading acute fear through my body. The click of the hammer cocking only makes it harder to gain control of the irrational emotion.

"It means he doesn't intend to accept my proposal." There are a few moments of silence as I quiver at the mercy of this sadistic criminal. "Why shouldn't I kill you right here and now?"

I look him in the eye. "Because I'm the best leverage you've got. Malachy's lack of response means nothing."

He holds my gaze and then releases the gun from my forehead and uncocks the gun.

I breathe a deep sigh of relief.

"You are right, but that doesn't mean I can't have some fun with you like he had with my wife." He puts the gun back into the holster at his waist before pulling out a knife. "Do you know what your brother did to my wife?"

The image of the scars on Aida flash into my mind. I shake my head. "I don't know half of what my brother does." I know Milo wouldn't be pleased that his wife had been speaking to me behind his back.

"He tortured her with a knife." He spins the knife in his hand. "One much like this."

I try to back away from him on the bed, but it's no use. The restraints hold me in place. "Please, don't."

Milo raises a brow. "Sorry, Alicia, but it's about time your brother paid for his actions." I watch as the cruel, unfeeling mob boss steps toward me with an evil glint in his eyes.

It's clear he delights in other people's suffering. A

man who is so utterly opposite to his wife, but they do say opposites attract. I bite my lip as he breaks open the buttons on my blouse enough for him to get access to the skin above my collarbone—the exact same place my brother maimed his wife.

He drags the blade hard enough to cut through skin, making me cry out in pain. It's excruciating—beyond anything I've experienced before. "An eye for an eye is a good philosophy." He forces my blouse further down my arm and cuts my shoulder in the same place Aida has a scar.

I grit my teeth and ignore the pain, allowing calming thoughts to flood my mind. It's the only way to survive this and I will survive it: me and my baby. My thoughts instantly turn to him—Niall, the love of my life. It was foolish to run from him the way I did, too scared to talk this through in the fear he didn't want a family with me.

Milo moves the blade against my throat, making me stiffen.

"Please, don't kill me," I murmur, fear arresting me. "I'm pregnant."

Milo stills, and I notice a flash of something in his eyes. It might have been guilt, but it was so fleeting I couldn't be sure. "I will not kill you, merely subject you to the same pain my wife felt."

He drags the blade lightly against my skin, cutting my neck, but not deep enough to break through any arteries. Once he's finished, he steps back and pulls a handkerchief from the top pocket of his suit jacket. He wipes my blood from the knife before stowing it back in the holster around his waist.

The thud of footsteps approaching catches both of our attention. The door swings open, and Aida stands there holding a bag of takeout. Her face pales as she stares at my wounds, glancing between her husband and me. "What did you do, Milo?" Her voice is bordering on hysterical at seeing the bloody cuts on my body.

"You shouldn't be here." His attention moves to the takeout bag in her hand. "What are you doing here, angel?"

She shakes her head. "You are as sick in the head as he is."

Milo growls softly, walking toward her. "An eye for an eye. It's simple." He grabs hold of Aida's hip and pulls her close. "Now, answer my question. Why are you here?"

Aida glares at her husband with such awe-inspiring strength. "I thought you wouldn't be back until tonight."

He tightens his grip on her hip and laces his other fingers into her hair, yanking hard. "Change of plan. Answer the question, Aida."

The only sign that Aida is scared is that her beautiful olive skin has paled. "You haven't fed Alicia once." Her eyes shift to me lying in the bed. "I have been feeding her while you are not here."

A beast-like growl tears from Milo as he grabs the bag from her hand aggressively, chucking it against the wall in a rage. He steps away from his wife. "You tried to undermine me. The concept of kidnapping is that your captor is supposed to suffer." He moves back to his wife and cups her face gently. "The way you suffered at the hands of her brother."

Aida shakes her head. "No, this barbaric behavior isn't acceptable. I would never wish what happened to me on any girl, no matter who she is." She goes over to the bag and retrieves it from the ground. "Alicia deserves to eat. It's a basic human right."

Milo rolls his eyes. "Don't start on me with rights again, Aida."

I find it hard to believe that these two are in a loving relationship. It's fraught, if you ask me. The way Milo speaks to her is disrespectful.

Aida ignores her husband and unfastens my restraints, leaning close and whispering, "They are here for you." She manages to salvage the veggie taco and places it into my hand.

I don't eat. I can't eat.

Hope coils through me, as she can only mean Malachy is here for me. I wonder if Niall is with him after the way I treated him. It wouldn't surprise me if he doesn't want anything to do with me anymore. Especially after the stunt I pulled, running away to New York City.

An ache in my chest ignites, overwhelming the

pain of the cuts on my body. Milo got his revenge because he inflicted the wounds on me that my brother inflicted on his wife. Now it's time to end this once and for all. Perhaps if Aida and I can talk some sense into the bloodthirsty men in our lives, we can all smooth this out without spilling more blood.

"Eat then," Milo says, his voice irritated as he moves toward me. "My wife has been kind enough to get you food, and I want to see you eat it."

Aida nods at me in encouragement, and I swallow my anxiety, forcing myself to eat the veggie taco. It's a bad idea to refuse to do what Milo says.

I hope that Malachy will steal me away from here sooner rather than later.

Milo turns to his wife. "We are going to have a serious talk when we get home."

I swallow hard, wondering if he will hurt his wife. "Please don't hurt her, she was merely being kind."

Milo growls softly. "I'd never hurt my wife. What do you think I am, a monster?"

Aida grabs his hand to calm him. "That is the way you've been acting. Why can't you and Malachy put this stupid feud behind you?"

He paces away from her. "Because neither of us are the type of men to back down, so how do you come to an agreement?"

Aida looks furious at that. "So, a fight to the death no matter who gets hurt along the way is the only option?" She shakes her head. "It's pathetic. Both of you are pathetic." She turns to walk away when the door swings open.

It feels like my heart swells the moment I see Niall. His ice-blue eyes find mine instantly and it feels like everything will be alright again.

Then, his attention moves to the bloody cuts on my body and anger so acute takes over his entire countenance. He tries to move toward me when Mal stops him.

Malachy holds his hands up in surrender, letting the gun he was holding drop. "Fuck, looks like we just walked into a damn trap." Both of their gazes move to Milo who has a gun aimed at my brother.

It feels like my world is spinning as I glance between the cruel Italian Don and my brother. They are so alike which is probably why they can't agree on a truce.

"Guns on the floor. Both of you," Milo growls.

Malachy and Niall place their guns on the floor before returning upright with their hands held high.

"Please, Milo. Listen to your wife," I press.

Milo's irritated glare moves to me. "Shut up. This is the perfect opportunity to end things once and for all." He steps toward my brother, who holds his hands up higher. "How did you find us?"

Malachy nods toward the poster on the wall behind me. "Rookie error, lad. I'd know that poster anywhere. It's a one of a kind."

My brother calling Milo a rookie only seems to

add fuel to the tension. He cocks his gun. "Well, look who the rookie is now. You've walked straight into my path so I can blow your damn brains out."

It feels like time slows as I notice Milo's arm tense, readying himself to pull the trigger. Panic floods me as I watch helplessly, unable to stop him from killing the man who has looked after me my entire life.

"Please, don't," I cry, but it is no use.

No one can reason with these men.

He pulls the trigger, and it feels like life as I know it is over. I'd rather be dead myself than live in a world without my brother.

## 26

## NIALL

*Five Minutes Earlier...*

Malachy leads the way as we walk toward Carnegie Hall, both of us on edge. The busy hustle of New York City dims in comparison to the frantic beat of my heart.

Adrenaline races through my veins as Malachy tries the door Aida disappeared through. It opens as she promised, giving us a way inside. If it weren't for her, this would be harder. I can't say I trust her one hundred percent, but as Malachy said, it's all we've got.

"Ready, lad?" Mal asks, setting his hand on the hilt of his gun.

I nod and do the same, ready to draw it the moment we're inside. Only a fool would walk into the enemy's lair without their gun drawn. Malachy steps inside first and I follow him, allowing the door to shut behind us.

It's dim inside the corridors of the famous events hall. We creep down the corridor toward the end and rest our backs against the wall.

"I'll check it's clear," Malachy say, before glancing around the corner. He quickly returns to the original position, shaking his head. Silence floods the air as we remain there, holding our breath as if it will save us from getting caught.

A man holding a machine gun walks past us and carries on straight ahead. He didn't detect us lurking in the shadows of the corridor off his left.

"Fuck, that was close," I whisper.

Malachy nods before checking the corridor again. "Clear." He points his gun in a motion to follow him.

We've been in some pretty crazy scenarios over the years, but this one takes the fucking prize. The Italians we are taking on right now aren't only led by Milo but by Enzo D'Angelo too. We're picking a fight with another organization which could cause us a world of trouble in the long run.

I follow Malachy into another dimly lit corridor until we get to the end. Aida's instructions on how to find Alicia were clear. We're almost there.

Malachy keeps his back pressed against the wall before glancing up and down the corridor. He sighs heavily and gives the signal to follow.

"Second door on the right," he murmurs, coming to a stop outside of it. "This is it."

The faint murmur of chatter comes from the room, no doubt Alicia and Aida talking. Malachy reaches for the handle and pulls it open. My eyes are instantly drawn to hers, and seeing her alive is the best thing I've seen all damn day.

Then, I notice the blood staining her white blouse and rage slams into me. Everything else pales as I walk toward her, but Malachy stops me in my tracks.

"Fuck, looks like we just walked into a damn trap." Malachy lowers his gun and holds his hands up in surrender.

I only then notice Milo standing in the corner with his gun pointed at us.

"Guns on the floor. Both of you," Milo growls.

I crouch down and place my gun on the floor. Malachy does the same. We stand and keep our hands up, facing the clan's number one enemy.

"Please, Milo. Listen to your wife," Alicia implores, pleading him with her eyes. I wonder what she means about him listening to his wife.

"Shut up. This is the perfect opportunity to end things once and for all." I hate hearing him speak to Alicia like this. Milo steps toward us. "How did you find us?" he asks.

Malachy nods to the poster on the wall. The one that gave it away. "Rookie error, lad. I'd know that poster anywhere. It's a one of a kind."

I think Malachy's word choice irritates him as he cocks his gun. "Well, look who the rookie is now. You've walked straight into my path so I can blow your damn brains out."

"Please, don't," Alicia cries, but as I look at the man with his gun pointed at us, I know it is no use.

The conviction in his eyes is certain. He intends to kill the both of us and end the war. I would expect nothing less from a man like him.

Alicia's screams fill my ears as the bullet tears through the air toward her brother.

It's as though time slows down as I force myself to move, leaping in the way of it as if my life depends on it, even though it's exactly the opposite. I could die instead of him, but that factor doesn't come into my mind.

All of us can see the trajectory of the bullet. If it hits, Malachy is dead. I think of nothing else but saving my best friend, no matter the cost. He sure as hell has saved me more than once.

The bullet travels through the side of my abdomen, making me wince. Blood sprays into the air as I force Malachy down with me. The impact hurts like hell, but he is safe.

Aida shouts at her husband. "What the fuck, Milo." She rushes toward him and grabs the gun out of his hand, holding it behind her back.

"Give me the gun, Aida," he says in warning.

She shakes her head. "Listen to me for once,

Milo." Her brow furrows as she glances over at Malachy and me. "Can't you see this is wrong?"

When Milo doesn't look at us, she nods at Alicia. "Look what you have done to these people." Aida takes a step away from her husband, backing toward the door. "You need to agree to a truce with Malachy." She glances at him lying on the floor next to me. "Both of you need to discuss this man to man, without your guns."

A vein in the side of Milo's head appears more evidently and his face turns redder by the second. "Aida Mazzeo. Since when do you give me orders, angel?" He walks forward, stalking her.

"I don't. I'm begging you to stop this before we all end up dead." Her eyes narrow. "This isn't the first time your war has put me in danger, and it won't be the last if you don't end it now."

Milo continues to close the gap between them before rushing at her. He isn't listening to Aida's logic. She escapes his grasp and turns around, sprinting out of the room.

The move takes Milo by surprise as he growls and takes off after her, leaving the three of us unattended in the room. The door is unlocked, meaning it's our chance to escape. Malachy and Alicia exchange questioning glances. Aida is giving us a way out, which makes no sense if she planned this.

"We better get out of here while we still can,"

Malachy says, helping me to my feet and supporting me.

Alicia comes to my other side and puts my arm over her shoulder too. She smiles at me, but it doesn't reach her eyes. I know that look. She scared we will not make it.

"Everything will be okay," I say to her quietly, wanting nothing more than to soothe her.

She shakes her head. "You don't know that."

I don't know it for certain, but I feel it in my gut. My injury isn't severe, even though I've lost a lot of blood. Somehow, we'll make it out of here alive and be together soon as a family. I lean against Alicia as she presses her hand against my wound, trying to stem the flow of blood.

"How much further?" she asks.

Malachy quickens his pace, forcing me to speed up despite the excruciating pain. "Not far. Keep pushing."

Every muscle in my body burns as I struggle to get enough oxygen into my lungs. The wounds I sustained from Milo's men before aren't fully healed and now this. My mind is racing as we turn the first corner, heading back to the exit.

"You are losing too much blood," Alicia says, panic in her tone.

I clench my jaw, forcing myself to take more of my weight. Alicia is struggling and Malachy can't exactly support me by himself. "It's a flesh wound, little lass. Don't worry about it."

Her brow furrows as if she doesn't believe me. I've been shot enough times to know the difference between a flesh wound and one that can cause serious damage. It was reckless to throw myself in front of that bullet, but Malachy was about to die. That's a fact I'm certain of. Malachy's brains would be splattered up the wall.

The thud of fast following footsteps echo behind us as we rush down the last corridor toward the fire exit which is lit ahead.

"Fuck, we need to get out of here fast," Malachy growls, taking more of my weight as he forces us to pick up the pace. "I know you've been shot, lad, but you need to help us here."

I groan. "I'm trying, boss."

I take more of my weight despite the agony and quicken my footsteps, knowing it's life or death at this point. Malachy still doesn't know that I lied about being signed off by Alastair.

Only one hundred yards left to go, as the thudding footsteps and men shouting gets closer still.

"Shit, we're not going to make it," Alicia says.

Malachy growls. "We will. Keep moving."

I'm not the only one with injuries. Alicia's bloody cuts are still visible as her blouse remains open, making me angry beyond belief. They may be superficial injuries, but I know she has them because of what Malachy did to Aida.

Malachy opens the door as the men chasing us round the corner. He let's go of my arm and Alicia helps me out into the street. Malachy opens fire in an attempt to hold them off. A bullet ricochets off the metal fire door, missing my head by inches. Malachy growls and fires more rounds, trying to slow them.

We rush toward the car across the street. Malachy follows us, slamming the fire door behind him.

Alicia opens the back door and forces me inside, making me groan at the pain shooting through my entire body. "Sorry," she says, buckling me into the backseat.

Malachy follows quickly behind us as he gets into the driver's seat.

"What is the plan?" Alicia asks, continuing to hold her hand against my wound. "If Niall doesn't see a doctor, he'll be dead before we make it to Boston."

That is true. If we don't stop the bleeding, I won't make it. However, I can't go to a normal hospital which makes this difficult.

Malachy meets my gaze in the mirror. "We can't take him to a traditional hospital."

Alicia shakes her head. "If a traditional hospital is our only choice, then so be it. Fuck the police or whoever else might question why he's been shot. He has to live."

I wish that were an option, but it's not. Not only is

a traditional hospital dangerous because of the police, it's easy for the Italians to find us. "It's not an option, Alicia."

"What are you saying?" she asks, searching my eyes with frantic desperation.

Malachy sighs heavily, rubbing a hand across the back of his neck. "I'm going to have to contact Devlin Murphy. He's the leader of the Carrick gang in New York."

*Shit.*

He must be desperate if he's thinking about contacting Devlin. Malachy pulls his cell phone out.

Alicia tugs at my arm frantically. "We need to get away fast; they are on to us."

"Shit," Malachy growls, turning the key in the ignition and firing up the engine. It roars to life as he puts it into gear and swerves onto the road, heading toward Brooklyn. We don't even know yet if Devlin will help, but he's our only option.

Malachy hits call and then puts the phone on handsfree. The dial tone fills the car as we rush away from trouble "Who is it?" a gruff voice answers.

"Devlin, it's Malachy McCarthy. I'm in New York and having some trouble with the Italians."

A few moments of silence pass by. "What do you want me to do about it, lad?"

Malachy's jaw clenches. "All I need is a favor. One of my men was shot and he won't make it back to

Boston. Can you give him shelter until he's back on his feet?"

I hold my breath, waiting to hear his response. "Sure. You know where to find me." He cancels the call.

I glance out of the back window and notice a blacked out SUV following us. "I think we've got company."

Malachy glances in the rearview mirror as he races away from Carnegie Hall. "The Italians shouldn't follow us into Brooklyn because the territory belongs to Devlin."

"How sure are you that we can trust this guy?" Alicia asks, continuing to hold a rag against my wound.

Malachy keeps his eyes on the road. "Pretty sure. He's Irish after all and hates the Italians." Malachy's eyes appear in the mirror. "If you hadn't taken that bullet, I'd be dead right now." There's raw emotion in his voice as silence floods the car.

A lump forms in my throat as I'd do it all over again. Malachy saved me all those years ago when he allowed me to tag along, and I owe him my life. There isn't a doubt in my mind that I wouldn't have lasted long alone on the streets. "It was nothing."

He shakes his head. "Only you would think taking a bullet for another person is nothing."

Alicia sets her hand on my face gently and looks into my eyes. "It was a reckless thing to do." Tears brim in her eyes as she moves her lips to mine and kisses me softly, unfazed by her brother being in the car.

"Alright, I've accepted you two are together, but I don't need to see it right now," Malachy growls, startling us both apart.

Alicia's brow furrows. "You told him?"

I swallow hard and nod. "I had to come clean to explain why you ran to New York in the first place." I meet Malachy's gaze in the rearview mirror.

Alicia glances at her brother. "I'm sorry it took us so long to tell you." She shakes her head. "I was scared you might kill him."

Malachy growls softly, keeping his eyes pinned to the road ahead. "Niall is like a brother to me. I'd never kill him, no matter how pissed off I am. I told you I'm done with that, Alicia. So, if Niall is the man for you then so be it."

Alicia smiles and squeezes my hand tightly as a comfortable silence fills the car. Malachy pulls into the outskirts of Brooklyn and as expected the SUV disappears. We've escaped, but the question is whether we're heading into another trap.

## 27

## ALICIA

The tension in the car is intense as Malachy parks opposite Devlin's townhouse.

"Are you sure this is a good idea?" I ask my brother, who continues to stare at the imposing building.

"It's our only choice," Niall replies. "I will go in there alone. There's less risk that way."

I tighten my grip on his hand, shaking my head. "No way. I'm coming in with you to make sure he is actually going to help.

Malachy remains silent, staring at the building as if lost in thought. A few more moments of silence pass as we all stare at the building.

"Alicia is right. I'm coming in there to make a deal with him to ensure your safety."

Niall shakes his head. "I won't let him rob you because of me."

The growl that comes from Malachy's lips is beast-like. "Do you really think there is any amount of money I wouldn't pay to save your life, Niall?" His eyes find Niall in the rearview mirror. "I would be dead right now if it weren't for you. I'd give that son of a bitch every penny to my name if it saved your life." There's raw emotion in his voice.

Niall chuckles, wincing as he does. "Well, don't let him know that."

Malachy shakes his head and opens the door, sliding out onto the street. I get out too and help Niall onto the sidewalk. His weight crushes me as I try to keep him upright by myself. "A little help here, Mal?"

Malachy takes the other side as we help him across the street toward the house. He stops in front of the door and rings the bell, glancing over at me. "Let me do the talking, okay?"

I clench my jaw and nod. "Fine."

A lady comes to the door and opens it. "You must be Malachy?" she asks, glancing right at my brother. "Come on in." She steps aside and allows us into his home.

A tall, muscle-bound man leans against the railings of the stairs with his arms crossed over his chest. "Long time no see, Malachy." He pushes off the rails and walks toward my brother, holding out his hand. "How have you been?"

Malachy takes it. "Could have been better. The Italians have been a thorn in my backside lately."

Devlin nods. "I heard."

"How have you been?" Malachy asks, irritating me that small talk is even a fucking option right now while the love of my life bleeds out.

"Better since the shit that went down with the Russians ended." He runs a hand across the back of his neck. "This is the man who needs a hand?" He chuckles. "You should have told me it was Niall. Of course I've always got space for him here."

A man holding a doctor's bag hurries up the corridor. "Sir, you needed me?" he asks.

Devlin nods. "Yes, take Niall and see that he is patched up and taken care off." He glares at the man. "Make sure you take good care of him, do you understand?"

"Of course, sir." He helps Niall down the corridor.

"What do I owe you for this?" Malachy asks.

Devlin shakes his head. "Nothing for now. If I need a favor, then you owe me one in the future." He glances down the corridor after Niall. "The both of you can wait here to see what his diagnosis is, but I need you to get out of New York as soon as we know."

My brow furrows. "Are you suggesting we leave Niall here?"

"I'm not sure who you are. Have we met?" Devlin asks.

I shake my head. "No, I'm Alicia McCarthy."

"Ah, the elusive sister." He takes my hand and kisses the back of it. "It's a pleasure to meet you."

I reclaim my hand. "Pleasure is all mine." Devlin seems like a friendly guy, but I wonder if it's all an act. These men are all the same: power and money hungry.

"Come, I'll take you to Niall's room where you can hear what the doctor has to say." He turns and follows down the corridor Niall and the doctor disappeared down. The woman who opened the door to us also follows. I can't still the erratic beat of my heart, anxious to hear the damage done by Milo's bullet.

Ever since we escaped Carnegie Hall, I haven't been able to get Aida's proposal out of my mind. I hope she's okay, considering Milo seemed pretty pissed at her attempt to undermine him. I think she has a point about us trying to find a way to end this war. If we don't then the people we love will end up dead. I almost saw Milo blow my brother's brains out.

Devlin opens the door to a medical room where Niall is lying on the bed with his shirt off. The wound looks terrible as the doctor cleans up the site. All I want to do is nurse him back to health. this, after all, plays to my expertise. The idea of leaving him in these people's care scares me.

"Is it a flesh wound?" I ask, walking up the doctor. "No impact on bone or organs?"

The doctor meets my gaze. "On first inspection,

yes. I need to run some tests and take an X-ray to ensure no shrapnel dislodged inside of him."

Niall grabs my hand. "I told you not to worry. I'm going to be fine." He winces as the doctor continues to clean the injury.

"There is an entrance and exit point, which means the bullet isn't inside of him. That's good news." He glances at Devlin. "I will need to monitor him for a week at least to be sure."

Devlin nods. "Fine. Both of you can return in one week to collect Niall."

The blood drains from my face at the thought of leaving him here alone for a week. "Can't I stay?"

Devlin shakes his head. "Sorry, lass. We don't want the Italians knowing we helped the McCarthy clan. It's better for us if we minimize the risk."

Niall squeezes my hand. "It's only a week, little lass." He smiles. "I'll be waiting right here for you." He pulls me close and cups my face in his large, warm hand. "I love you, Alicia."

I feel a lump form in my throat as I lean forward, pressing my forehead against his. "I love you too. Get better for me."

He nods. "I promise."

Malachy clears his throat. "Enough of that. Come on, Alicia. Let's get out of here while we still can."

I kiss Niall briefly before following my brother out of the room. It's hard to walk away from him, especially when all I want to do is remain by his side. "I hate this," I murmur.

"You and me both, Sis." Malachy looks guilty as he gets to the front door, glancing back at Devlin who followed us. "Thanks, lad. I'll be back in one week exactly. See you then."

Devlin nods in response and watches as we leave his home, shutting the door behind us. I feel so hopeless as I leave the man I love, abandoning him in New York City.

One week can't pass by fast enough. Niall and I have a lot of things to talk about, but more importantly I just want to hold him and never let go.

---

One week later...

Malachy paces the room, waiting to see Niall.

It was too risky to take him to a hospital within Enzo's territory, but thankfully Devlin Murphy agreed to help. I know that if we had waited and taken him back to Boston, he might have died. Even so, I hated leaving him here alone. It felt wrong.

"What the fuck is taking so long?" Malachy murmurs to himself.

I walk toward my brother and set a hand on his shoulder. "Calm down, Malachy."

He meets my gaze. "Niall saved my life. I left him

in the hands of a man who cares about nothing but himself."

Someone clears their throat behind us. "Thanks for the vote of confidence, lad." Devlin stands there with his arms over his chest before stepping aside. Niall walks into the room, looking better than I expected considering the amount of injuries he has sustained lately.

"Yeah, Devlin did good. You need to give him more credit where it's due," Niall says.

I rush toward him and wrap my arms around him, gripping him as if my life depends on it.

He chuckles. "Did you miss me, little lass?" Niall asks.

I feel tears prickle at my eyes as I continue to hold him, feeling his powerful arms wrap around me in return. He brings his lips to my ear and whispers, "As I missed you, baby girl. So damn much."

My chest aches hearing him say that. There's so much left unsaid between us ever since I walked out on him at The Three Amigos. We need to talk about everything, but right now, all I want to do is hold him.

Malachy clears his throat. "Alright, lad." He claps him on the shoulder, forcing him to let go of me. "I owe you more than I can ever repay," he says, pulling Niall into a hug.

Niall shakes his head. "Don't mention it." He pauses a moment, glancing at me and my brother.

"Just say that you are fine with Alicia and me being together."

Malachy's jaw clenches, and he meets my gaze. "This is what you want, isn't it, Alicia?"

I nod. "So much."

He smiles. "Then, of course, who am I to say no to my best friend and sister being together?" His expression turns serious as he looks Niall in the eye. "I can't think of a better man for Alicia, just make sure you protect her."

Niall nods. "Always."

Devlin Murphy claps his hands. "As great as this soppy reunion is, can you have it outside of New York City?" He runs a hand across the back of his neck. "The last thing I need is to get on the wrong side of the Italians right now. I had enough shit with the Russians last year."

Malachy nods and walks toward him, taking his hand. "Thank you. If you ever need a favor, don't hesitate to call on me."

Devlin shakes his hand. "If we can't rely on our own people, who can we rely on, aye?"

"Thank you, Devlin," I say, walking toward the man my brother spoke so badly of. I hold my hand out and he shakes it.

"No worries, now get out of here."

I reach for Niall's hand, and he wraps an arm around me as we walk out of Devlin's house.

"How have you been, baby girl?" he asks.

I shake my head. "Worried sick about you." It's the truth. I've hardly been able to sleep not knowing how he was doing in Devlin's care.

"You shouldn't have been. I've been treated very well here." He squeezes my hand. "We have a lot to talk about."

I meet his gaze. "Yes, but not right now." The thought of discussing anything with my brother present makes me uneasy.

"Would you two keep up?" Malachy calls.

We hasten our pace as he rushes out, where his man has the car running still. It was one of Devlin's requests that we get into the city and out quickly. He doesn't want Enzo knowing that he helped us escape, as it could cause tension between his gang and the Italians.

It's crazy how much shit I've learned about the underground world my brother functions in during one week. After being held captive, it became clear that although Malachy has protected me from it, I've never stuck my neck out and asked about it. Ignorance is bliss, but it's dangerous in this world we live in.

I open the back door to the town car and help Niall in, following him to sit by his side.

My brow furrows when Malachy goes to close the door. "Aren't you getting in?"

He shakes his head. "I'll ride up front with Rory." His brow furrows. "Something tells me you two need time to talk, but that better be all you do back here." His nostrils flare as he gives Niall a warning glare that could chill most hearts.

"Aye, sir," he replies, smiling. "Thank you."

Malachy shakes his head. "No, thank you, Niall." He shuts the door and gets into the front, which is shielded by a privacy screen.

Niall rests his head back, looking utterly exhausted.

"I don't think you should go back to work for a long while." I rest my hand gently on his chest. "You're clearly a magnet for bullets."

Niall opens one eye to glance at me. "I can't sit around doing nothing. I'll go crazy."

I smile. "I'm sure I can help out with that."

He shakes his head. "Alicia, I'm so sorry for the way I reacted when you told me that you are pregnant."

"It doesn't matter. All that matters is we're both alive and together again."

He sits up straighter. "It does matter, because I do want to have a family with you."

My chest aches hearing him say that, but I can't help but wonder if he's only saying it to appease me. All I know is I can't live my life without him. "You know you will make an amazing dad, right?"

His brow furrows. "I'm not sure about that, little lass."

He's crazy if he thinks otherwise. "You have

always protected me, ever since we met. A man who cares as much as you do has to make a good father. Especially when you take care of me so well."

His eyes brim with unshed tears and he shakes his head. "I never had a good role model though."

I cup his face in my hand. "That's exactly why you will be so good at it. You know what makes a bad father and will do anything to be the opposite." I press my lips to his, kissing him passionately. "I love you, Niall." I kiss him again. "I love you so much it hurts."

He grabs hold of me and forces me to straddle his lap, wincing a little as he does. "I love you with all my heart. Always have done and always will, little lass." He kisses me again, deepening it this time.

We stay in that position, kissing the entire way back to Boston, both of us lost in the utter bliss of our love, cocooned in it's safe embrace, knowing that everything will be okay as long as we have each other.

28

NIALL

*One Month later...*

The rush of cars overhead brings me right back to that day.

"Niall, what is going on?" Alicia asks, her blindfold still firmly fitted in place.

I tighten my hand on her hip. "You will see shortly, little lass." I lead her to the spot where we first met, knowing that for us there is no better place to do this. It may not be traditionally romantic, but it feels right.

I position Alicia in the spot where she lay next to Malachy, before leaning on the concrete column where I first spoke to her. "You can take it off now."

Alicia's throat bobs as she reaches for the blindfold and tugs it away. She smiles when she sees me, then I notice recognition dawn. Tears flood her eyes as she clutches onto her chest, doing a twirl to take in the cold, concrete underpass where we first met. "This is where we met," she says, almost in disbelief. "How did you find it?"

I shrug. "I never lost it, little lass." I step toward her, feeling my heart pound hard in my chest. Although we were kids, I think my soul recognized hers the moment we met. We were destined to end up here, together with a baby on the way.

"Why are we here?" Alicia asks.

I smile and cup her cheek in my hand. "So many questions." I press my forehead to hers. "Can you believe how long it took us to hook up?"

Alicia sighs. "No, it feels like we've wasted so much time."

I capture her lips with mine, reveling in my woman's softness. "That's why we have no time left to lose." I fiddle with the velvet box in my pocket, knowing that it's now or never.

"What does that mean?" she breathes, asking me yet another question.

I take a step away from her. The box in my hand feels heavy as I drop to my knees, feeling more vulnerable than I've ever felt. "Alicia, I can't spend one more day without you by my side." I lift the box and flip open the lid, revealing a cushion cut diamond engagement ring. "Will you marry me?"

Alicia's mouth falls open, and she stares at me in shock, clutching her chest. A few long moments pass by, and she still says nothing.

I clench my jaw. "A yes or no right about now would be helpful," I say.

She shakes her head, making disappointment spread through me like a disease. "Sorry, I'm in shock." Tears flood down her cheeks. "Of course I'll marry you." She steps toward me and helps me back to my feet.

I smile and remove the ring, putting it on her ring finger. Once on, I pull her close and kiss her as if it's the first time. The swelling sensation in my chest is overwhelming, making me certain I've never been as happy as I am in this moment.

"I love you," I murmur, breaking the kiss and holding her face in my hand again. "I love our baby too."

Alicia's tears flood down her cheeks. "Are you sure about this, Niall?"

I chuckle. "Surer than I've ever been." I tug her closer again, wrapping my arms around her waist. "The question is, are you sure?"

Alicia tightens her grip on me. "Absolutely."

I feel the unconquerable need for her taking hold of me as I grab her shoulders and move back enough to look into her eyes. "I need to have you, now," I breathe, moving my lips to her neck and nibbling on her sensitive flesh. "You are everything to me, Alicia." I unbutton the front of her blouse, pressing kisses to her chest. "Always have been and always will be."

Alicia shudders, eyes closing as I move the cup of

her bra down and suck on her hard nipple. She moans, spurring on that primitive need to fuck her here, the place where we first met all those years ago.

I lift her and carry her to the grass verge, setting her down gently. Without saying a word, I lift the hem of her skirt and groan when I see she isn't wearing any panties. "Good girl," I murmur before sucking her clit into my mouth.

Her hips buck and she laces her fingers in my hair.

I work my tongue into her tight pussy, tasting her deeply. Her taste calls to me in the most fundamental way. I slide my finger into her cunt, fingering her as I lavish all my attention with my tongue to her pleasure center.

"Fuck, daddy," Alicia moans, moving her fingers to her breasts and playing with her nipples.

The sight motivates me as I continue to drive her toward her climax. My cock throbs in my taut boxer briefs, leaking into the fabric. The rush of the cars on the highway above only spur me on as the light of the day fades over Boston.

I suck her clit forcefully, and it's all she needs to tumble over the edge. Alicia's body shudders beneath me as I lick her through it, lapping up every drop of her precious juice.

My cock pulses in my boxers as if it has a life of its own, demanding to be freed. I reach down and unzip my pants, freeing it without removing my clothes. "It's time for you to taste me, baby girl," I say, standing with my legs on either side of her and crouching in front of her mouth so my cock touches her lips. "Suck it."

Alicia obeys, opening her mouth to allow the length of my cock to slide into her throat. She gags slightly, but the more we practice, the better she gets at deep-throating me.

I thrust in and out of her, fucking her throat viciously as a mix of saliva and precum spills down her face. "That's it, baby girl. Take my cock in that pretty little throat," I growl, unfazed by where we are.

I don't care right now if anyone sees us. All I care about is claiming my fiancée. It's hard to believe that she's agreed to marry me. She's agreed to be mine forever, until death do us part.

All those years that I watched her from afar, obsessed with my best friend's sister, there was never a time when I truly believed we'd end up together. Hell, if someone told me we'd have a family, I would not have believed it.

Time has made it easier to come to terms with becoming a parent.

Alicia grabs hold of my thighs, trying to gain some kind of control as my cock chokes her.

I pull my cock from out of her mouth, giving her chance to breathe. "Do you enjoy choking on my cock, little lass?"

Her eyes are dilated as she wipes the saliva from

her mouth seductively. "Not as much as I love swallowing your cum, daddy," she answers, making me crazy with lust.

"Open wide then," I growl, sliding every inch back into her throat.

She gags at the force, but I can't hold myself back. I lose all control as I fuck her throat like an animal, chasing my climax with no regard of anything else.

I feel it slam into me as I roar, shooting down her throat.

Alicia swallows every drop as I pull my cock from her mouth. She even grabs my cock and licks the cum from the tip, making me crazy. It's all it takes for me to remain as hard as nails.

I move to between her thighs and rub the head of my cock through her soaking wet center.

Alicia watches me with lust-filled eyes, her lip quivering in anticipation as I hold her gaze. "Are you ready to be filled in both holes?" I ask, since I put the butt plug in her before we left the house.

She moans. "Yes, daddy."

I shove my hips forward, taking her in one stroke.

Her muscles tense around me, and I can feel the huge plug filling her asshole and pressing against me. It's tight as hell. We've worked her up to the largest plug now, which means she's ready for my cock next.

"Fuck, you are tight," I growl.

Alicia runs the tips of her fingers over my chest, feeling my muscles as they contract. "It feels so good being stuffed in both holes," she moans like the good little submissive she is.

"You are such a good girl, Alicia," I murmur, moving in and out of her with slow, careful strokes. "You take my cock so well with that plug in your ass."

Her eyes roll back in her head as I accelerate my thrusts, fucking her harder and faster with each one. It's beyond belief how well my little lass takes such rough sex.

I groan as her muscles spasm in record time, warning me she's about to come. The flood of hot juice against my cock almost tips me over the edge, but not yet. "Fuck, I love it when you squirt all over my cock," I growl.

Her eyes clamp shut as she revels in the euphoria, looking goddess-like with her dark, curling hair splayed out over the grass.

"Time for me to fuck your pretty little ass for the first time," I growl.

Alicia licks her lips as I flip her over onto all fours, tapping the handle of the plug wedged in her tight hole.

We've been working up to my cock, but now is the time I'm going to make her experience the length and girth of a real dick inside her most intimate part.

I pull a small bottle of lube out of my inside jacket pocket, a bottle I carry everywhere in case the opportunity arises for some fun when we're out together.

"Are you ready, baby girl?" I ask, thrusting two fingers into her dripping wet cunt.

She moans, head lulling forward. "I've never been more ready. Fuck my ass, daddy."

I stroke my cock in my hand before gently pulling the huge plug from her ass. The sight of her hole gaped for me, ready to feel my cock is almost enough to destroy me.

I squirt lube onto her hole, working it in with my fingers. Next, I lather my cock in it. This is the first time any man has ever fucked her in the ass. It's my privilege to take her anal virginity and be the only man ever to venture there.

The thought drives me wild as I align the head of my cock with her still gaping asshole.

Alicia moans the moment she feels me against her skin, nudging at her entrance. "Fuck my ass, please."

I push through her muscles, stretching them more than they've ever been stretched.

Alicia half moans and half cries as I slide deeper, letting her feel every inch as I claim her pretty ass for the first time.

"That's it, baby girl. I want you to take every inch." Her hole clings to me so damn tightly it feels like it was made to fit my cock.

Alicia groans. "It's too damn big."

I dig my fingertips into her hips, slowing myself down. "Tell me if it's too much and I'll stop."

She shakes her head frantically. "No, don't stop."

Her voice is a desperate rasp that sets my soul soaring.

I clench my jaw and allow the last two inches to disappear inside of her, closing my eyes as the pleasure is almost unbearable. "Damn, that feels like heaven."

Alicia whimpers below me as I pull out, watching as her tight little hole clings to me as if desperate to pull me back inside.

Slowly, I work her hole until my cock slides in and out freely.

Alicia's pussy juice drips down her thighs as I fuck her ass. It's a pretty fucking picture, watching as she takes it so well.

I grind my teeth and force my hand into my jacket, pulling out the vibrator I carry with me.

Alicia moans at the mere sound of the vibrations pulsing through the air. "Oh, God," she cries as I press it to her clit.

Her body tremors as I continue to fuck her ass, increasing the pace with each thrust. Her clit feeling the vibrations as I turn it up, wanting to feel her climax with my cock buried in her ass. "Take my cock," I growl, thrusting in and out of her ass roughly.

If it weren't for the rush of cars speeding over us on the highway, I would have forgotten we are outside entirely. I'm lost in us. Lost in the thrilling sensation of loving this woman with every part of me.

Alicia's back arches, giving me the angle to sink even deeper inside. "I'm going to come, daddy," she cries.

I grind my teeth together as a flood of liquid squirts from her delicious pussy, followed by spasms deep within. My cock throbs deep inside her ass as I continue to fuck her through her third orgasm. The tight grip of her asshole makes it impossible to hold out any longer.

The climax that hits me is aggressive as I roar against Alicia's back, biting her shoulder to stop myself from being so loud the whole of Boston would hear me. Every thrust drains more of my cum deep in her ass.

We're both panting and out of breath as we come down from our mutual pleasure. I finally pull my cock from her ass before plugging it with the anal-plug again. "I want you to keep my cum in your ass, baby girl."

She turns around and kisses me. "Yes, daddy."

I groan and deepen the kiss. I could spend eternity under this underpass, losing myself in my soul mate. When we break the kiss, I notice we have an audience. "Looks like we got caught, little lass."

She glances over at a couple of scruffy looking homeless men and her nose wrinkles. "Gross."

I pull her skirt down and grab my jacket, wrapping it around her shoulders since I broke the buttons on her blouse earlier. "Let's get out of here."

She nods and takes my hand as we walk back to my car, parked just off the verge.

I open the door for her before walking around and sliding into the driver's seat. "I think it's time to celebrate our engagement." I reach into the back seat and grab the new dress I purchased for her. "I got you a dress and I've booked a table at your favorite place."

Alicia smiles. "The Three Amigos?"

"Where else?"

The smile on her face is enough to lighten my life in ways I never believed possible. I know without a doubt that I'm the luckiest man in the world to have found the other half of my whole. Alicia is definitely my soulmate in every sense of the word.

# EPILOGUE

## ALICIA

*Seven months later...*

Niall presses his lips to my huge baby bump, making me smile. "Hey there, little guy, how are you tonight?" he asks.

The baby kicks and I'm sure he has to be ready to come out anytime. I'm due in a week and so is Scarlett, which is crazy.

*What are the odds that my brother and I would become parents at the same time?*

I can't deny that the idea of Malachy being a father isn't one I ever considered. He'll make a good one because of his savagely protective nature, but he never struck me as the fatherly type. However, seeing the way he is with Scarlett makes my heart happy. It feels like finally the three musketeers are getting their happily ever after.

"He's a fighter, just like his dad," I say.

Niall kisses me softly, sending shivers down my spine. We've been careful when having sex; no rough play since he found out about the baby, but he's still as insatiable as ever. "Have you heard that sex can move the process along?" he asks.

I laugh. "That's convenient, isn't it?" I sigh heavily. "My feet are aching like hell."

Niall is quick to grab them and give me a massage, taking care of me every step of the way. "How does that feel, baby girl?" His fingers work out the tension expertly. There's no doubt that he's been more attentive during this pregnancy than I ever expected, especially considering his initial reaction to the news.

"Good." I wince as a cramping pain hits me again. "Fuck, I keep get these damn contractions."

Niall raises a brow, fingers stilling on my feet. "Is the baby coming?"

I shake my head. "No, Alastair said they are Braxton-Hicks contractions. They are so damn painful."

"So no sex tonight, then?" he asks.

I shrug. "I'd never say never." A terribly painful contraction hits me, and then a flood of liquid follows, drenching the bed.

Niall's eyes widen. "I think your water just broke."

"Shit," I say, gripping hold of the bedding as a painful contraction tears through me. "That hurts."

"Okay, hold on. I'll ring for Rory to bring the car

around right now." He dials the number on his cell phone, looking calm considering the chaotic throughs racing through my mind right now.

"I need the car outside in two minutes, lad."

His brow furrows. "What? Are you serious?" He laughs. "Alicia has just gone into labor too."

My eyes widen. "No way."

"See you in a minute." He cancels the call. "Scarlett went into labor as well."

I shake my head. "What are the odds?"

"Pretty fucking slim, but it's happening. Rory is already outside with the car waiting for them." Niall helps me off the bed. "Time to go."

I wince as another contraction tears through me. "Damn it." I clutch hold of Niall's hand as he leads me out of my room and down the stairs.

"It's going to be alright, baby girl. We'll get you to a hospital in no time," Niall reassures me.

We make it out of the house to find Malachy helping Scarlett into the back of the town car. He turns when he hears us. "I can't fucking believe it. Rory just told me." He shakes his head. "Looks like we're doing this together, aye?" He claps Niall on the back. "How you holding up, Sis?"

I glare at him. "Just get me to a hospital, this hurts like hell." My brother never has been great in crises like this.

Scarlett cries out in the back of the car, and he pales, rushing to sit by her side. I can't deny that it warms my heart seeing the way she transformed my cold-hearted brother into a caring, doting boyfriend. It's kind of amusing.

"Oh fuck," I say as another contraction makes me double over in pain. "Get me to that damn hospital, now."

Niall helps me into the other side of the town car before sliding in next to me. He grips my hand so hard it hurts, but it's a welcome pain as it's a distraction from the contractions.

Scarlett meets my gaze across the seats. "I can't believe we're doing this together."

"Me neither."

She cries out as a contraction hits her. Out of everyone in this goddamn car, only she knows the hell I'm going through. "It hurts so damn bad, doesn't it?"

Scarlett nods, trying to steady her breathing as my brother clings to her as if she's going to break.

"It's going to be okay, darlin'," he murmurs, moving his fingers in soothing circles over her thigh.

She leans her head back against the headrest and shuts her eyes.

Another contraction hits me and it's the worst one yet. "Oh, fuck," I cry, clinging onto Niall's hand so hard he groans.

"Damn, you have a powerful grip, little lass," he says, squeezing back. "Hang in there. We'll be at the hospital in no time."

I need to be on some damn pain meds already. Damn Alastair and his Braxton-Hicks theory, it made me dismiss the real contractions. I had planned to be on fucking painkillers by this point of the pregnancy.

I breathe in and out calmly, trying to quiet my mind as Rory pulls the town car in front of the hospital.

Niall releases my hand. "Wait here and I'll grab a wheelchair."

Malachy does the same as they both rush together to grab one each, leaving Scarlett and me hyperventilating through the pain.

They both return and help us out of the car into the wheelchairs, pushing us into the ER waiting room. Malachy goes up to the desk while Niall waits with us. I grind my teeth together, trying not to cry out from the pain.

Scarlett cries out as another contraction hits her, but hers seem to be further apart than mine. "I need some pain meds right now," she says, glaring at Niall.

Niall pales at the ferocity in her expression. "Malachy is sorting it. Hold on."

Malachy returns with two paramedics who take control of our wheelchairs. "We are taking you straight to the maternity ward to check how far along you both are," one of them explains.

The paramedics rush us to the maternity ward. From the closeness of my contractions, I can tell I'm almost ready to deliver. Scarlett, on the other hand, isn't having them as frequently.

"Good luck," I shout to Scarlett as she veers off into a room on the right. Malachy rushes in right behind her, staying with her every step of the way.

Niall chases after us as they take me into the next room on the right. "Is she ready to deliver?" he asks.

"We don't know, but her contractions are close together." He positions me in the room and a woman walks in. "How long ago did your water break?" he asks.

I glance at Niall, unsure of how long it's been.

"About half an hour now," Niall says.

He nods as he reaches between my legs to check how dilated I am. It's ridiculous when I see Niall's fists clench at the sight of him touching me there, especially considering the circumstances. He says nothing as the man stops, shaking his head. "I think you are going to be very lucky. You are ten centimeters dilated, which means the baby is ready to come already."

I huff a long breath, shaking my head. "That means it's too late for pain meds?"

The woman steps in. "Unfortunately, yes."

"Fuck," I curse, irritated that I have to do this with no fucking pain relief. "Let's get this over with."

Niall squeezes my hand tightly, and I look into his eyes, knowing in that moment that everything will be okay. It may hurt like a bitch, but we'll make it through this. The woman places my feet into stirrups, forcing my legs open. The doctor sits on the bed. "Now, I want you to push for me and make sure you keep breathing deep breaths."

Niall keeps hold of my hand as I start to push, groaning as I do. The pain is excruciating as the doctor keeps telling me to push. It goes on for what feels like an eternity, constantly pushing through the agonizing pain.

"You are doing great," the doctor says in encouragement. "A few more pushes and you will be there."

The promise of an end to this painful experience drives me onward as tears spill down my cheeks. I squeeze Niall's hand so hard he makes a squeaking sound as I push again, taking deep rasping breaths of oxygen between each push.

"Come on, once more. The baby is almost out."

I grit my teeth together and push for the last agonizing time, growling as I do.

The sound of crying quickly follows, sending relief through every part of my body. I relax against the pillow, thankful that it's finally over. All my energy is utterly spent as the nurse takes my baby to clean him up.

"You've got a very healthy baby boy," she says, returning with him swaddled in a blue blanket. She places him in my arms and suddenly my exhaustion melts into the background.

I hold our baby in my arms, feeling in awe at the

unexplainable love I feel for this small, defenseless person. A person who Niall and I made.

Niall kisses my forehead, staring down at me with the same devoted love I feel in my heart. "I love you both so much it's hard to believe I won't explode." He places his finger into our baby's hand. "We haven't even chosen a name yet."

I smile at him. "One name I've had in mind for a while. Aidan, after Aida." I shrug. "She saved all of our lives."

Niall smiles and nods. "I love it. Aidan Fitzpatrick it is." He presses his lips to Aidan's head. "Welcome to the world, little lad." I know without a doubt that this moment is the happiest of my thirty-eight years of life. Malachy appears in the doorway, looking exhausted. "How's my nephew? I just heard you gave birth." His brow furrows. "They think Scarlett has a couple of hours yet."

I feel for her hearing that as I could not put up with that pain for that long. "Aidan Fitzpatrick," I announce, smiling. "Do you want to hold him?"

Malachy nods and moves forward, taking Aiden into his arms. The look in his eyes is one of pure love. "Hey little guy, your cousin is going to be here soon."

I squeeze Niall's hand and rest my head back on the pillow, breathing a sigh of relief. A year ago, I never could have imagined life would be so blissfully happy as it is now. Niall and Aidan are my world, and I can't wait to live the rest of my years with them.

THANK you for reading Vicious Daddy, the fourth book in the Boston Mafia Dons Series. I hope you enjoyed reading Niall and Alicia's story.

The next book in this series follows the brutal bratva pakhan Mikhail Gurin and Siena's story in the fifth book of the series, Wicked Daddy. This book will be available through Kindle Unlimited or you can pre-order on Amazon.

Wicked Daddy: A Dark Captive Mafia Romance

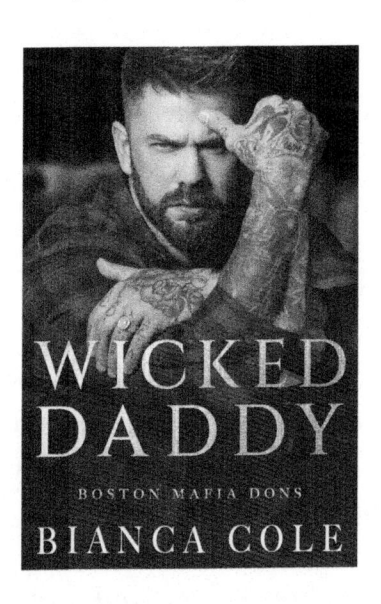

**Christmas vacation with my two best friends turns into a nightmare I never saw coming.**

Aida and Gia begged me to vacation with them in

Boston. My parents were away in Hong Kong, so I agreed. It might be one of the worst decisions I've ever made.

I'm snatched from the bar we're drinking at. Taken captive by one of Milo's enemies. The Russian Bratva boss, Mikhail Gurin.

He holds me for ransom in an attempt to force Milo to back down from a merger. Milo doesn't strike me as the kind of man that accepts threats. It means I'm doomed to a fate worse than death.

Mikhail Gurin is brutally handsome, but he's as wicked as sin. The way he looks at me scares me to the core. He intends to use me as his slave and plaything until Milo submits. He tells me he will ruin me for all other men and then toss me aside.

Milo will never back down, so it means I'm entangled in this trap forever, destined to be used by the Bratva boss for all eternity. Will his wicked ways ruin me forever?

**Wicked Daddy is the fifth book in the Boston Mafia Dons Series by Bianca Cole. This book is a safe story with no cliffhangers and a happily ever after ending. This story has some very dark themes that may upset some people, hot scenes, and bad language. It features an over-the-top possessive, and wicked Russian Pakhan.**

# ALSO BY BIANCA COLE

**The Syndicate Academy**

Corrupt Educator: A Dark Forbidden Mafia Academy Romance

Cruel Bully: A Dark Mafia Academy Romance

**Chicago Mafia Dons**

Merciless Defender: A Dark Forbidden Mafia Romance

Violent Leader: A Dark Enemies to Lovers Captive Mafia Romance

Evil Prince: A Dark Arranged Marriage Romance

Brutal Daddy: A Dark Captive Mafia Romance

Cruel Vows: A Dark Forced Marriage Mafia Romance

Dirty Secret: A Dark Enemies to Loves Mafia Romance

Dark Crown: A Dark Arranged Marriage Romance

**Boston Mafia Dons Series**

Cruel Daddy: A Dark Mafia Arranged Marriage Romance

Savage Daddy: A Dark Captive Mafia Roamnce

Ruthless Daddy: A Dark Forbidden Mafia Romance

Vicious Daddy: A Dark Brother's Best Friend Mafia Romance

Wicked Daddy: A Dark Captive Mafia Romance

**New York Mafia Doms Series**

Her Irish Daddy: A Dark Mafia Romance

Her Russian Daddy: A Dark Mafia Romance

Her Italian Daddy: A Dark Mafia Romance

Her Cartel Daddy: A Dark Mafia Romance

### **Romano Mafia Brother's Series**

Her Mafia Daddy: A Dark Daddy Romance

Her Mafia Boss: A Dark Romance

Her Mafia King: A Dark Romance

### **Bratva Brotherhood Series**

Bought by the Bratva: A Dark Mafia Romance

Captured by the Bratva: A Dark Mafia Romance

Claimed by the Bratva: A Dark Mafia Romance

Bound by the Bratva: A Dark Mafia Romance

Taken by the Bratva: A Dark Mafia Romance

### **Wynton Series**

Filthy Boss: A Forbidden Office Romance

Filthy Professor: A First Time Professor And Student Romance

Filthy Lawyer: A Forbidden Hate to Love Romance

Filthy Doctor: A Fordbidden Romance

### **Royally Mated Series**

Her Faerie King: A Faerie Royalty Paranormal Romance

Her Alpha King: A Royal Wolf Shifter Paranormal Romance

Her Dragon King: A Dragon Shifter Paranormal Romance

Her Vampire King: A Dark Vampire Romance

## ABOUT THE AUTHOR

I love to write stories about over the top alpha bad boys who have heart beneath it all, fiery heroines, and happily-ever-after endings with heart and heat. My stories have twists and turns that will keep you flipping the pages and heat to set your kindle on fire.

For as long as I can remember, I've been a sucker for a good romance story. I've always loved to read. Suddenly, I realized why not combine my love of two things, books and romance?

My love of writing has grown over the past four years and I now publish on Amazon exclusively, weaving stories about dirty mafia bad boys and the women they fall head over heels in love with.

If you enjoyed this book please follow me on Amazon, Bookbub or any of the below social media platforms for alerts when more books are released.

Printed in Great Britain
by Amazon